CW01642130

The Supplanter

By the same author

Flaming Janet
Shadow of Palaces
Marjorie of Scotland
Here Lies Margot
Maddalena
Forget Not Ariadne
Julia
The Devil of Aske
The Malvie Inheritance
The Incumbent
Whitton's Folly
Norah Stroyan
The Green Salamander
Tsar's Woman
Homage to a Rose
Stranger's Forest
Daneclere
Daughter of Midnight
Fire Opal
Knock at a Star
A Place of Ravens
This Rough Beginning
The House of Cray
The Fairest One of All
Duchess Cain
Bride of Ae
The Copper-Haired Marshal
Still Blooms the Rose
The Governess
Children of Lucifer
Sable for the Count
My Lady Glamis
Venables
The Sisters
Digby
Fenfallow
The Sutburys
Jeannie Urquhart
The Woman in the Cloak
Artemia
Trevithick
The Loves of Ginevra
Vollands
A Dark Star Passing
The Brocken
The Sword and the Flame
Mercer
The Silver Runaways
Angell & Sons
Aunt Lucy
O Madcap Duchess
The Parson's Children
The Man from the North
Journey Beyond Innocence
The Charmed Descent
The Inadvisable Marriages
Curtmantle
Murder in Store

The Supplanter

PAMELA HILL

ROBERT HALE · LONDON

First published in Great Britain 1998

ISBN 0 7090 6330 X

Robert Hale Limited
Clerkenwell House
Clerkenwell Green
London EC1R 0HT

2 4 6 8 10 9 7 5 3 1

Typeset in North Wales by
Derek Doyle & Associates, Mold, Flintshire.
Printed in Great Britain by
St Edmundsbury Press, Bury St Edmunds, Suffolk.
Bound by WBC Book Manufacturers Limited, Bridgend

PART 1

1

A FAIR-COMPLEXIONED man of thirty-two was running fast through woods he knew well. Despite the fact that lately, in the way of his family, he had begun to put on flesh, he moved swiftly and his breathing did not quicken. His long dark hair, of whose thickness he was proud, fell forward as a rule over his forehead, but to allow freedom of action he had tied it back, hunter's fashion, with a thin leather thong. Knowing his way, he continued swiftly between the young trees of the late king's New Forest, planted a generation ago where there had formerly been hamlets; the trees by now were thick with August leaf, and appeared to harbour neither man nor wolf. The runner made his way with the speed and precision of an athlete, his pale face hardly deepening in colour. Prince Henry, brother to the present king, had run fast and often from a boy. It had frequently been necessary by the time he became a man.

His eyes, grey in colour and said as a rule to be gentle and pleasant in expression, were for the moment hard and unyielding as iron. Henry was remembering, with a bitterness hoarded over the years, how in youth, in this very forest, they had mocked him, all of them, for not having enough money to own a horse. He, the Conqueror's youngest born and, in his own opinion, only rightful prince, had had to demean himself by following the royal hunt on foot, like a servant. 'Deerfoot! Hartfoot!' He could hear the jeering voice of Warren and Surrey, his cousin, now, being himself well mounted then. By this time, they were after the same bride. It made today's plan more urgent still.

That was not all. At their father's death, after the Conqueror's horse had bucked at a burning faggot in a French street, injuring the corpulent old man by thrusting him hard against a spiked iron pommel, the Conqueror had expressed a dying will which Henry resented fiercely. Rufus, Henry's immediate elder, had always been their father's favourite; no doubt the Conqueror had retained a certain innocence as a result of many years of happy marriage, and perhaps considered that a son of his who had fathered no bastards was pure in his manner of living. The notion of a sodomite would have repelled him; and even Henry had not dared tell him the truth. The ring had been taken from the dying finger and sent with Rufus to claim England, although Henry himself had been born there, alone among them all, in the year after Queen Matilda had crossed over from Normandy to visit her husband in his new kingdom won at Hastings.

As for the duchy of Normandy, it had gone to Robert Curthose, the remaining eldest, whose squat figure and undoubted charm had made him best loved by their tiny mother, so much so that in the end it had led to a quarrel between her and her husband. Curthose would not make an able ruler; he was self-indulgent and constantly in debt.

However it was the question of England which had inflicted the deepest wound; and when it turned out that he, Henry, would receive only five thousand marks and no land, he had almost burst out in anger at the deathbed itself. He had made them weigh out the exact sum in silver before his father's eyes, thereby bringing a gleam of humour to those at the last. 'Wait, and by the end you will inherit all,' the old duke-king had murmured; then had died.

Henry reminded himself that he had been the only son dutiful enough to see his father buried, though the body had been despoiled by servants when it had been left for a short time alone. Later, the Conqueror's corpse had burst in the too-narrow grave they had prepared for it in Caen abbey, making an unforgettable stench in course of the requiem.

Much of the five thousand marks had been borrowed by the ever-needy Curthose; Henry had exchanged it for land in the Vexin. Later, Curthose had taken back the land without repaying the money. This had justifiably led to war, in which Rufus had joined. By now, they had made outward peace, the three of them; and Curthose was far away. Henry sneered; Curthose had chosen to take the cross, abandoning his duchy. By now, he was on the way home.

All of that – and Henry's mind, precise as a clerk's, forgot nothing – must be set aside for the moment. What had to be done now took precedence over everything else, even the intended future.

He had earlier asked the king and his minion Tirel for a private word, away from the others in the party. After both had gone off he had murmured to the rest that he himself ought to go to have his bowstring tied at one of the remaining cottages. They might think what they liked of a recent warrior who couldn't tighten his own bowstring; and he had made straight for the appointed place, a certain landmark oak. Presently, when there was a stag – these abounded still – the pair, his brother the king and Tirel close by as always, would come at a gallop down the cleared way. He, Henry, was already standing behind the oak ready to take aim, and not at the stag. He held ready one of the six sharp arrows brought to the king that morning.

'Give me one to try, brother,' he had said to Rufus, who with his usual unthinking generosity had handed one to Henry and one to Tirel. He had then jested to the latter about not missing his mark.

That was helpful; such things perhaps signified approval from an all-seeing God. If he himself were to miss his mark, there was no harm done. If his arrow found its target, by night he would be king of England.

It had paid, therefore, to be in time, and allow his hands to grow steady. Despite everything they were still a clerk's, white and soft. Henry thought of the past while he waited. Rufus, king now, had been from birth their father's favourite: Robert, the eldest after Richard's death, their mother's as stated. He, Henry, born last of all the family, and in England at that, they had tried to turn into a monk. The prince's eyes narrowed. He'd shown even his determined father, in the end, that he was in no way monkishly inclined. He had called his eldest bastard Robert, after the Conqueror's father. Meantime, the monastic schools had taught him the art of writing in a fair, clear hand on vellum; an accomplishment seldom met with in princes. It would be of use when he was king.

Henry squinted through the leaves at the sun; it was almost time. The moment, the only favourable one since the Conqueror's death thirteen years ago, must be seized without fail. Robert, the eldest surviving heir whom their father had called Curthose in mockery because of his short legs (but he had left him Normandy) was on the way home from Jerusalem with a rich young bride. He had, rumour said, refused the crown of the new Christian kingdom carved out with much bloodshed, saying he preferred to wait for the crown of England. It was known Rufus would never marry, unless . . .

Henry thought of the exception, and the grey eyes grew ugly. William Rufus, second of the name in England, had been to take a look at Eadgyth Matilda, princess of Scotland, shortly after she was brought south as a fugitive to the convent at Romsey on the deaths of both her parents. Eadgyth – he himself must induce her to use the second name, his mother's – was descended from the old Atheling line of royal English kings, which made her a desirable bride, although penniless at least till matters were settled again in the north. She and her younger sister Mary were, accordingly, so much sought after that their aunt Christina had transferred them to Wilton, further away from lascivious Norman suitors residing in Winchester or even – his sister Constance's hopeful widower, Alan Fergeant, had made a proposal for Eadgyth already, but had not been considered – from Brittany, which called itself a dukedom if no longer a kingdom.

The refusal had been made in the time of Eadgyth's late father, King Malcolm Ceann Mór, perhaps according to the wishes of his much-loved wife. Margaret Atheling, queen of Scotland, had evidently had an ambition for her children denied to herself; all her sons must become monks and both her daughters nuns. The sons had, to a certain degree, fulfilled this obligation; but the girls were highly marriageable. There was however the aunt to overcome; she was Margaret Atheling's sister, and the girls' guardian now that both their parents were dead in memorable circumstances.

Henry had made a point of visiting Wilton convent for himself, though not in his own sole company: he had been careful to be escorted either by Eadgyth's young brother David, who after a rival had seized Ceann Mór's throne had been brought south by an uncle for safety and reared at the English court. The uncle also took part, somewhat odd as he undoubtedly was. Edgar the Atheling, by descent rightful heir of England, would, had he had an ounce of spirit of ambition, have secured the crown for himself before old Edward the Confessor died in the year of Hastings. As it was, even the Conqueror had considered the Atheling so harmless he might be let live.

He and his sisters had escaped, in the end to Scotland, where

Margaret had duly married the widowed king. By now, Edgar could lead in any company to a convent of high-born young women without objection even from the Lady Christina Atheling, Edgar's other sister, a redoubtable lady not yet abbess.

Unfortunately, the second earl of Warren and Surrey had also taken it into his head to call at Wilton.

Henry scowled. The earl had made the excuse of visiting his own sister Edith, who was being educated there since their parents had likewise died. However the earl had strong ambitions to gain the crown for himself, with supposed rights through his late mother. That must neither be dwelt on or allowed; one's eldest sister Gundreda, barely remembered, had been dead now fifteen years. The earl was in any case too prone to delay in all he did, never making up his mind one way or the other. He had not yet, as far as one knew, proposed for the Scots princess. He must be caused to look elsewhere. *Deerfoot, Hartfoot*. One had not forgotten.

Henry took time, while waiting by the oak, to think briefly of Eadgyth Matilda herself. Before seeing her he had expected either a convent mouse or an uncouth Scot, but she was neither. Apart from being able to hold her own against the formidable aunt in an unavowed silence, she seemed mannerly; one need not be ashamed of her in front of the English court. No doubt she had learned proper behaviour from her mother, who had not, after all, died till Eadgyth was fifteen. Queen Margaret Atheling had been accustomed to life in palaces in Hungary and in England, to which last she had been returned from exile as a child. King Edward the Confessor and his queen, Eadgyth Godwinson, had reared her and her sister and brother, presumably filling their heads with piety as well as manners.

Later, in Scotland, Margaret had made an energetic partner for the Scots king, and had carried out certain church reforms there which had not made her altogether popular. Such matters would not concern her daughter. He, Henry, would be master in all such situations: he thought quickly of one which was pending.

Nevertheless besides being an asset to any candidate for the crown of England, Eadgyth Matilda was Curthose's god-daughter, which explained why she bore their own mother's name as well as that of the late Confessor's queen. Curthose had chanced to be in the north at the time of the Scots princess's christening, and after building a fortress he called Newcastle, had enjoyed brief amity with King Malcolm and his wife; he made friends easily. Despite Margaret Atheling's initially expressed intention of taking the veil rather than marry, she had rewarded her devoted king with six sons and two daughters, presumably telling the sons they had best not imitate their father. So far the sons had been obedient; none were married.

Henry reflected that if nobody bred, there would be no continuity of a royal line; that had happened in the late Confessor's instance, he having taken a vow of chastity. (It would hardly be advisable for oneself, and in any case was too late). However an unaccountable affection seemed to linger among the Saxons here for their old line of kings; to marry Eadgyth Matilda was a sure way to their loyalty. He, Henry, had already quietly cultivated the name of Atheling for himself; it meant the heir, and reminded those who needed reminding that he had not only been born among the English, but was the only one of the Conqueror's sons to be conceived in full wedlock. His parents had waited in vain for papal permission to marry, then had gone through the ceremony without waiting any longer. It was even possible – there had been great fondness between them – that Gundreda by then was already on the way.

The thought of her reminded him again of her son, Warren and

Surrey. How cumbersome that title was! It had been Rufus, not the Conqueror, who had bestowed it on the earl's father, for services in the early rebellion in the first year of his reign. Then, also, half the nobility, including old Bishop Odo, the Conqueror's half-brother, had wanted Robert Curthose to inherit England as well as Normandy. Curthose was certainly more of an immediate danger than Warren. The present duke of Normandy would bring with him not only the rich southern bride, but the powerful reputation of a soldier of Christ. Getting on for fifty though he was, Curthose would father heirs; one of his bastards, also named Richard – it was a name of the old dukes of Normandy, and like Curthose to bestow it on some casual woman's son – had been shot down here with an arrow in exactly the same manner as the prince his namesake, their brother, some years before. It didn't do to put it into the heads of the common people, even now, that Norman princes were easily to be slain with arrows.

It had been given out, when the Conqueror's first son died, that Prince Richard had succumbed to marsh fever caught in one of the forced clearings made when they planted the king's new forest. Curthose's bastard's death it had not been thought necessary to explain. The first slayer, a Saxon, had privately admitted to the prince's killing, but had evaded punishment by entering a monastery. Nobody had admitted to the second murder, and nobody – Henry smiled – would admit to the third.

He had made war on his two brothers in Normandy after their father's death, and after they had made war on each other. Curthose, good-natured spendthrift that he was – the new young duchess's dowry wouldn't last, the present duke had borrowed and spent their mother's money before she died, and he, Henry, had himself as already recalled lent Curthose a part of his own legacy from their father, making it a condition that he received the Vexin, the debatable land on the edge of France. His scowl deepened. But for that, he would be landless.

Kindness didn't pay. Curthose never failed in it. When he, Henry, had been trapped at last by both brothers on the high sea-girt rock off Brittany, where they said the archangel Michael had landed long ago from the air, there had been no water. Rufus would cheerfully have let Henry and his following die of thirst, but Curthose had said 'We have but one brother left', and had sent up not only enough water, but a cask of wine. In the end they'd all made peace, and he himself had returned, under a slight cloud, to England and Rufus's court. This land, which should be his – he was, he again reminded himself, a prince born in England, the Atheling – still lay sullen and passive after the Conquest, though the new king, despite his many broken promises ('What man can be expected to keep them all?') – seemed to get on well enough with the common people, who of course knew him well by sight.

Rufus was difficult to forget, with his shock of saffron hair and his red face, and the pot belly, these days, of the ale-drinker. The Saxons called him the Red King, and liked him without trusting him. Reasons for the death could be advanced. They could blame Tirel, who wouldn't be able to answer back; or else say the king himself had been a willing victim, by arrangement, to the old forest gods. It was a pregnant date and the new century, and William Rufus had reigned thirteen years. He had never made pretence of being anything but pagan; had refused, at his coronation, to take the sacrament. He, Henry, would make sure all things were as they ought to be at his own crowning. Except for Scotland, where they still relied on anointing on a cherished stone, a crown, by now, made a king.

Henry stared on beyond the thick immemorial trunk of the oak. It had stood there since long before the Confessor's reign, perhaps before that of Alfred.

Henry pricked his ears; there was a stag coming at last. It

shouldn't be long now until everything was over; or, rather, about to begin.

Not far off, hidden likewise among the trees and keeping as still as a tree himself, a second man was watching. Of a different breed from Prince Henry, he knew the king's youngest brother by sight well enough. He himself was a charcoal-burner, and witnessed many things that happened here. It was best these days to keep quiet, whatever you saw. These Norman bastards would have your eyes or your right hand, or failing that your testicles, if you got yourself noticed. If it came to a choice, he, Purkiss, supposed he'd lose the last and keep his sight and livelihood. He had two young sons at the other side of the forest, having married late, not that his old mother knew. He still lived with her for her protection, and for a bit of peace. His wife's family wouldn't take to do with his mother, calling her the priest's whore. That was unfair. She and his father had been married, granted by the skin of everyone's teeth, before he himself was born; and although his father had been trained in Latin at King Edward's monastery school in Winchester as a boy, and had meant to be a priest, he'd lost the notion when they started forbidding priests to marry, saying it wasn't natural. An order from overseas, that had been. Them as kept strict ways kept them, while others didn't; and so if he himself wanted to visit Gifu and his children it meant a six-mile walk across what had once been the hamlet clearing, busy with folk. Now, it was full of the Conqueror's damned plantings, grown into trees. Everyone who'd lived all their days in the hamlets had had to crowd in elsewhere as best they might. Gifu's folk were among them, having seen their dwellings razed; but his mother's cottage hadn't been, his father having ended as a charcoal-burner and in the end so had he. The Norman invaders needed charcoal for their braziers, in the castles they'd built to defend themselves.

He was as good as any Norman, and better; he had a name. Purkiss didn't sound much, but it had come down from the time of the Roman legions. His father had told him it had once been Porcius, which was the name of a very ancient Roman family indeed, before the emperors. One of them, a famous soldier and scholar called Cato, had drunk nothing but water all his days. He, Purkiss, however liked his ale. Both his mother and Gifu brewed it well; but as for taking a hare for the pot, that wasn't safe any more, as it had been in King Edward's day. There had been mutilations lately because a deer was found drowned, let alone if one was brought down for meat. King Edward wouldn't have permitted that.

Purkiss could just remember seeing, as a boy, the old Confessor riding past at speed, white hair and beard flying; besides being a monk despite his wife, as they said, he'd been a notable hunter, with his good face grown rosy with the wind. It was a pity he'd thought fit not to father sons; church orders again, no doubt. It had caused a deal of trouble, and much death, ever since these foreigners came. They'd altered everything, not only the forest laws; there was no freedom now, like there had been since King Alfred won it back from the Danes long ago. Small wonder two of the young Norman princes had been slain with arrows here, among the trees.

Purkiss's eyes narrowed, and fixed themselves on the waiting figure of Prince Henry. *He* hadn't shot the first lad, that had been done by the Saxon who'd taken the cowl; but Henry's own nephew on the wrong side of the blanket was a different story, having been shot from behind an oak like the one Prince Henry stood at now. They hadn't said too much about either death, knowing there was resentment over the razing of the hamlets. Nevertheless he, Purkiss, knew what he knew, and had seen what he'd seen; and Prince Henry didn't know he was being watched again now, standing ready with his arblast and arrow. Duke Robert was abroad; it could only be one more target now, the king himself. A poor charcoal-burner had best know nothing.

Purkiss and Henry both heard the thunder of an approaching stag at last. Purkiss stared down at his own bare arms, grimy with wood-ash below his rough tunic. Henry sited his bow, arrow poised at the ready.

Henry could smell the stag's acrid odour as it came; its nostrils flared, its eyes glinted red with challenge and fear. It had flung its head back, so that the antlers brushed the branches; it was a buck of the first head. He noted such details coldly, his mind clear, waiting for the hunters who must soon follow. They came in sight, the king foremost, cap jaunty as usual with its heron's feather, saffron hair flying beneath, like a banner. William Rufus's knees gripped his mount: he was laughing, with the excitement of the chase and with the pleasure of the company of Tirel, whom he loved. Henry's mouth pursed. Walter Tirel rode slightly behind, tight-laced like a woman. His profusely curled long hair had been tied back for the chase. He had a wife and children in Normandy. Henry let fly the arrow from his bow, viciously and with precision.

He heard the twang, saw the great stag buck and rear – he'd grazed it slightly, a near thing – then he forgot it, thrusting off as it did among the branches. The arrow had found its mark, straight into the heart of the oncoming king. William Rufus, second of England, dropped from the saddle without a cry, the stain already spreading over his green tunic and the pot belly beneath. The forest gods he worshipped were silent. Tirel on the other hand had already begun a high keening, like a woman. He flung himself from the saddle and knelt beside his master, seeing the red face already whiten, the eyes remaining open. Rufus spoke his last words in a low voice.

'Make off, Wat. Get to Normandy.'

His head fell sideways then and the other scrambled up, sobbing, mounted his horse, and rode away. The king lay, still bleeding, on the ground. The stag had gone.

Henry himself had wasted no time, but hastened back to where the others waited. He strolled towards them, smiling. He felt a compulsion to boast; the plan had succeeded.

'I have been some time,' he said. 'I had to find a cottage where they might tighten my bowstring, as I said. There are few to be found now. The woman there told me an extraordinary thing. She said I would be king before sunset.'

He looked at the others; they included his friend FitzHamon, but also William of Breteuil; the last had never liked him. De Breteuil thought a good deal of himself, no doubt, being the son of Proud Spirit of Hastings, who had urged on the assembled baronage of Normandy to follow its duke across to England for what they had considered a mad adventure in 1066. But for that, they might none of them be here. He saw the others grow restive shortly, waiting for the return of the king and Tirel. 'You had a word with the king, had you not?' said de Breteuil. He used no title, which angered Henry.

'I could not find them,' he replied with equal discourtesy. Time passed and in the end, a search was begun; no doubt the stag had taken the king and Tirel further off. Henry made pretence to search among the rest, but kept near his horse.

Finally there was a shout from among the trees.

'He is here. He is hurt. Come.'

The king's body had been found, the sharp arrow still in its heart; the arrow given to Tirel that morning, sharp and notably crafted. Tirel had fled; that was a sign of guilt. It had no doubt been an accident; the arrow might have glanced off the stag, or an oak; no matter. There was a search for a cart to take away the body, from which the blood still gouted unaccountably. By the time they found the charcoal-burner, Prince Henry had gone. With a few poor folk following on foot who had heard the rumour that the king was dead, a king who had always spoken to them cheerfully despite his faults, William Rufus was conveyed for the last time to Winchester. Already his brother was riding there at full gallop; with de Breteuil grimly close behind.

Henry went straight to the castle, demanding the keys to the treasury. 'The king is dead,' he told them, adding that there had been an accident. De Breteuil came up as he received the keys, demanding them in his turn loudly in the name of his liege lord, Robert of Normandy. By that, Henry knew Rufus was dead; he himself had not waited to be quite sure. If they had pulled out the arrow, that would finish the matter. Meantime, de Breteuil must be dealt with. Henry drew his sword. A small crowd had gathered, and he addressed them in his clear deep voice, which few could resist and the sound of which made men afraid.

'I and no other am your liege lord,' he said. 'I am the Atheling, the true prince born in England, the only one born in full wedlock after the pope approved my parents' marriage. I and no other am England's king.' He promised them better laws, as his brother had done without carrying the matter out.

There was a mixture of cheering and some hostile shouts. The latter were quenched by Henry's friend, a second Henry, de Beaumont of Meulan, earl of Warwick, who laid about him with the flat of his sword, silencing any who spoke out of turn. In the end Henry won the day, and those who had cheered followed, taking time to stare at the lolling body of Rufus as it was brought in on the cart. The rest departed for their own safety. The blood still dripped, soaking the ground beneath; women were screaming. De Breteuil had been taken away. 'Bury my brother tomorrow,' said Henry, 'with a hunter's mass. There was no priest by him at his death.' The blood could soak on into the earth, and be forgotten.

He knew that he must appear to defer to the ancient rights of the Witan, and had it put about that as many as could be assembled at Winchester had voted for him. In this he was helped by a further member of the family of Beaumont, to whom he would always continue to be grateful; the father, known as Robert of Meulan although he had a right to the Leicester title, owning much land there, had been an adviser of Rufus, and his prudent face was welcome at one's own council table although he was not in good health. His second son, Warwick, who had persuaded those who disagreed at Winchester, ensured that thereafter he and his brothers were much in Henry's favour.

Crowning was the next essential thing; a crown made a king; it could not be set on Henry's head by the archbishop of Canterbury, because that saintly prelate, whose name was Anselm, had quarrelled with the late Rufus and had gone abroad to Bec. There was no time to wait for his return. Henry was anointed by one bishop and crowned by another, the ailing bishop of York: he felt the welcome trickle of the sacred oil on his bare flesh, as had happened since the time the Caesars made themselves gods; and the reassuring hardness of the gold circlet Rufus had occasionally worn was presently pressed on his own brow. He felt no particular emotion, not even triumph. He was shown to the people, who, still bewildered at the turn of events, obediently cheered the tall figure in its long new robes of state, with the gleam of gold about the dark long-haired head. The Atheling, as he called himself, was king. They accepted it meantime, and King Henry again promised to govern well, but so had his brother done; it mattered little who ruled them by now.

Among the reminders of old Saxon ways present was a lame noble, Simon de St Liz. He had long ago wanted to marry the widow of Earl Waltheof, the last Saxon earl; but she would not have him, and instead he had been given her young daughter. Henry noted Simon's presence idly; he would be a supporter: and, himself, meantime created new bishops. He also sent word to Archbishop Anselm to hasten back to England. His presence would lend legality.

2

EADGYTH MATILDA was jumping on her black horsehair veil. The stuff was of a nature to survive this treatment, which happened whenever Eadgyth was left alone: or, rather, in the company of her young sister Mary. Being princesses, they were not obliged to sleep in the common dorter, but were permitted to share a cell.

That was the only privacy. It was no better and no worse than Romsey, which they had left four or five years ago. The Lady Christina, their aunt, was not yet abbess in either place, but was given full authority owing to the present real holder's great age and frailty. Ordering everybody came by nature to Christina Atheling now that they were no longer in Scotland, the king and queen there, Eadgyth's parents, being both dead.

Eadgyth stared down at the veil, which she hated for what it signified. Her father the king, when she had been about ten years old, had torn one off her head when her aunt Christina, who still lived with them then, had put it on and bidden her pray. 'No daughter of mine will become a nun,' King Malcolm had sworn, and Eadgyth could remember his stalwart figure as a rock against which she could lean. Her mother had been beautiful, energetic, and pious; but King Malcolm had had a poem sung about him by a Gaelic bard, which Eadgyth still remembered.

A king, the best who possessed Alban;
He was a king of kings fortunate.
He was the vigilant crusher of enemies:
And there shall not be born for ever one who had more fortune and greatness.

There was a great deal more of it. She remembered the singing cadence of the Gaelic, which one never heard down here.

She remembered other things. She had been fifteen years old when she sat beside her dying mother in Edinburgh Castle, near the little stone chapel her father had built for his wife and to which Queen Margaret Atheling went daily when she was in health. Now, though, King Malcolm and Eadgyth's eldest brother Edward were away fighting in Northumbria, and her mother had fallen ill.

Slowly, she had died, and just before that happened news had come that the king and his heir were dead also. Eadgyth's two next brothers, Edgar and Ethelred the abbot, had carried Queen Margaret Atheling's body out of the castle secretly, in a thick mist which had come down, lest her enemies – as a Sassenach, a Saxon woman who had tried to change their ways, Queen Margaret had enemies – insult it; and having covered the beautiful dead face with a linen cloth, conveyed the body to Dunfermline.

That had been done by the two of Eadgyth's brothers who like herself had Saxon names: another, Edmund, had betrayed them. She and Mary and the two youngest boys, Alexander and David, had been hurried south by their uncle Edgar Atheling to Romsey convent, where by then the Lady Christina was, having herself taken the veil. They would be safer there than in Scotland, where another had meantime seized the throne; but the Lady Christina was concerned about the approaches of suitors for Eadgyth, and had made the girl wear the horsehair veil always: in fact, would have turned her into a nun if she could, and beat Eadgyth frequently for refusing.

Eadgyth loathed the veil; for one thing its shape was like a coffin. On the way down they had ridden through the desert which the Conqueror had in his time made of Northumbria; charred remains of forgotten villages jutting up through the high weeds that had grown, in a generation, through the scorched earth. The bones that had been left to whiten had, by now, been buried; the monks who guarded the body of St Cuthbert at Durham, to which it had been returned after many wanderings, had buried the dead as they might, over time. Yet the place had a bleak forsaken air Eadgyth could never forget. This was the place where her father had met his death, by treachery; and her eldest brother Edward had died two days after, of his wounds. She remembered them often in her prayers, and her mother.

'One day it'll burst its seams,' said Mary in reproof about the veil. She was not yet old enough to be made to wear it. Eadgyth kicked the offending object further off along the elegant stone floor which had replaced the former earth one. Shortly before their day, the late Confessor's queen, after whom she was named, had rebuilt Wilton in stone, in emulation of her pious husband's great new abbey at Westminster. There were comforts, therefore, suitable for the daughters of noblemen, even princesses.

However daily life was simple. Their pallets lay side by side in the cell, their few clothes in a chest by the wall below the crucifix. Mary at least would not remember having more; but Eadgyth herself recalled splendid furnishings at Dunfermline, the place her mother had turned into a court as grand as any, even making King Malcolm, who left to himself took things as they came, wear royal gear when he went out among the people.

She remembered many things of the kind. There had been the great jewelled cross Queen Margaret had brought from Hungary, with an ivory figure of Christ and an immense diamond. It lay in a black case when not in use and was called the Black Rood. The palace, and the chapel Queen Margaret had built, were hung with bright tapestries and embroideries, some of which Eadgyth had been allowed to help make. By now, both her parents were buried together in the chapel. It was fitting that, having loved each other greatly in life, they should have died within four days of each other; the queen, having been ill, had herself died at news of the king's murder at Alnwick. Everything seemed planned. It had been the will of God which long ago had driven Margaret Atheling and her family ashore on the Firth of Forth in a strong storm, instead of being borne back to Hungary when the Conqueror took the English throne.

He had permitted them to depart, but could not have foreseen the Scots marriage next year. 'The mountains of Abernethy defeated him,' Eadgyth recalled her father saying, smiling above his grey beard. He had been somewhat older than her mother, and a widower when she came. She herself hadn't known her half-brother, Duncan, her father's eldest son who had been kept hostage in England, and who had been murdered almost as soon as he went north to reign. It was safer here. Alexander, her second youngest brother, had returned to Lothian when he was old enough, to help the rest fight. David was still too young, and lived at court; now and again he came to visit her, with her uncle Edgar Atheling or with others.

Eadgyth curled up on her pallet and thought of the others, in particular Earl Warren and Surrey, with his smooth yet hesitant manners. He had said that he wanted to marry her, but that it would take time to arrange. Eadgyth considered the situation, and if it would be better or worse than the one she was in at present. She had no particular feelings about Warren and Surrey, although his sister Edith, who spelt her name in the Norman fashion, had been friendly before she left Wilton to be married to a Norman knight, Gerard de Gournai. Once they had come back, Edith dressed in the height of fashion, with leather shoes that curled upwards at the toes, and a laced bodice; they were going together to the Holy Land to rescue the tomb of Christ, with the great pilgrimage which included Duke Robert Curthose of Normandy, Eadgyth's godfather.

If Earl Warren had shown signs of going on the pilgrimage, Eadgyth almost thought she would have gone with him, not only to escape from aunt Christina but to ride, like a few other hardy women, with her husband to free the Holy Sepulchre in Jerusalem from the infidel. However the earl had stayed at home, and that was three years ago. The Christian armies had meantime taken Jerusalem, there had been miracles like the finding of the Holy Lance at Antioch, and now many were returning home, while others stayed on in what was to be a new kingdom.

Edith herself had come back with a different husband; Gerard, like so many, had died abroad. Edith had come to Wilton and described the splendours of the emperor Alexius' court at Constantinople, and his scholarly daughter Anna who was writing her father's life, and the round beaded cap the emperor wore, with long dangling pearl earrings, as his presence was supposed as far as possible to denote the splendour of God.

Eadgyth sighed. Everything seemed to be happening outside the walls of Wilton. She had been almost five years in convents now; she would like to be free. Events in the world beyond had been happening even before the time of St. Edith, who had refused to become abbess here at Wilton at the age of thirteen, and had then died of consumption. She had been the bastard daughter of King Edgar the Peaceful, sent here as a baby: they said she had never known the world, so could not have left it. She, Eadgyth, greatly wanted to know the world; even, perhaps, still as the bride of Earl

Warren, who grumbled that he had some right to be the next king as his mother had been the Conqueror's eldest daughter, given to his father as a reward for aiding Duke William in Normandy, long before Hastings.

Meanwhile, her own favourite place in the chapel was beside the tomb of the little saint, who was said to have sat up and slapped the face of the impertinent King Cnut when he had her coffin opened during his reign to see if she was really incorrupt after a hundred years.

'You are silent,' said Mary, who liked to talk, if only in whispers; anything louder was disapproved of here and might bring in an angry aunt Christina, with her rod.

She appeared in the doorway now, frowning, one hand having jerked aside the curtain. The years of deliberate penance had set Christina Atheling's face in harsh lines. At Wilton, where young girls of noble birth were sent to be prepared either for marriage or the cloister, she was respected but not loved. She watched her elder niece scramble up from the pallet.

'Put on your veil, Eadgyth. You should treat it with more care than leaving it lying on the ground as you do. It is almost time for the evening office. That is better. You should not slouch in idleness, but behave with more decorum; your saintly mother desired you both to take vows, as you know, and you are a bad example to Mary.' Mary was more tractable, and needed reproof less often, also less use of the discipline; the princesses' mother had told their tutors, in her time, not to spare the rod, and the Lady Christina seldom failed to obey this behest, less for the girls' good than because she herself felt thwarted. Eadgyth's soft mouth was mutinous now.

'My father King Malcolm desired that we should not take them. For myself, I have no vocation, and should not be forced.' Of this

Eadgyth was certain; she loved the things of God, but not as a nun, and there was no alternative but marriage.

'You are pert in your replies for a penniless orphan. You are fortunate in that this distinguished convent will accept you without a dowry, because of the endowment the late queen made.' Eadgyth had been named for the Confessor's queen, whom Christina herself had met again on her earlier way south, once more encountering the devout lady who had brought her up with Margaret and Edgar from childhood. It was true that this girl now, Margaret's elder daughter, was devout and said her prayers; but rebellion must be rooted out. Even the way Eadgyth stood at present, as though she owned the cell, was less respectful than it should be. Unfortunately she had grown almost as tall as oneself, like a young plant, and her reply was one more proof of her regrettable state of mind. It was as well Edith de Warenne had left to be married long ago, with her worldly chatter; and male visitors of course were worse, but one could hardly prevent the girl's brother and uncle from calling to ask how she and Mary fared. Christina heard her niece's quiet voice now with rising anger; a girl of her age should by no means answer back in so calm a way.

'Both Mary and I are eligible to marry well through our descent, which like your own is of the house of Cerdic and the old English kings. The king here now came to ask for me at Romsey, and you let him think then that I was a novice.'

'The king here is not fit for any self-respecting girl to marry; you should be grateful to me for protecting you from infamy.' She declined to describe the infamy; the known habits of King William Rufus were unfit to occupy a place on any gently reared woman's tongue or in her head. 'Prepare yourself for the office within the quarter-hour, and try to humble your will. It is grown harmful to you,' she said, and turned to go, dropping the curtain.

At least she didn't beat me today, Eadgyth Matilda thought with relief; it was true that Our Lord had suffered stripes with patience, as Eadgyth tried to remember when it happened. She had already put on the loathed veil, and spread out its stiff folds evenly. Its presence would certainly discourage any man who did not know who she was.

She had of course been made to wear it on the day King William Rufus came to Romsey. She had been younger then, perhaps still almost boyish in appearance. She had heard the Lady Christina's strident voice, so different from her dead sister the Scots queen's, ushering in a visitor. 'Come and see the roses in my garden,' Christina Atheling had been heard to say.

There had been no roses at that season; she meant her novices. Eadgyth Matilda had been made to pass by among these, wearing the great ugly veil. On passing she had ventured to raise her eyes. A stocky man with a red face and yellow hair was standing there, staring at her as far as it was possible to do so; his eyes held a kind of puzzled appeal, as if she, Eadgyth, could help him in some way. She had never refused help to anybody, whatever nature this might take; but the Lady Christina had made a sharp gesture with her hand, and Eadgyth had lowered her gaze obediently and had passed on with the rest. Afterwards her aunt had sent for her, giving her three blows with the discipline across the shoulders.

'That is to make you remember not to behave in a forward fashion before men. You will forget this visit of the king's; he is not interested in young women. You must wear the veil at all times. It is for your protection as well as to signify what you are to become.'

It was soon after that, perhaps because of it, that they had removed to Wilton. The king hadn't come back again; no doubt he had decided she was a nun. If he hadn't been interested, why had he ridden to Romsey? However Wilton was much further away.

Time passed, and there were other visitors, including the king's youngest brother Prince Henry.

He had been brought the first time by her uncle Edgar Atheling, and David her own youngest brother had come. David was beginning to learn Norman ways at court and to speak French rather than Gaelic. Eadgyth's uncle the Atheling was unchanged; he was ageless, like an elf, neither old nor young, in some way not like other people. She could remember her father King Malcolm fitting out a fleet, with gifts and armour, to help his brother-in-law the Atheling regain the English kingdom that was his by right: but a storm had sunk the ships and all the gear. That was the kind of luck Edgar the Atheling had; but in any case he would doubtfully have won against the Conqueror, by then firmly ruling England. Eadgyth recalled her father's anger at news of the sinking of the fleet, which had cost him a great deal of money and trouble: and her mother putting her white hands against his tunic and kissing him, to take away his temper as she well knew how to do.

'You have done your best for all of us,' she had said. 'Rest now; be content in my love, and in the children.'

He had growled that a storm had after all brought her to him, which was fortunate, and maybe this one was a sign that he ought to do as she said; and after that the Lady Christina had returned to England and taken her vows, and they had all been happy together in Edinburgh and Dunfermline until disaster came. Now, David was talking about life at Windsor and Woodstock, and the tall dark-haired man who had come with him sat silent for the most part, assessing Eadgyth with grey eyes that held a pleasant and gentle expression, as by custom when Prince Henry wanted something.

3

KING HENRY commenced his reign with ruthless swiftness, knowing exactly what he had to do; firstly, to obtain the fealty of certain strong barons, even for the time being and for the sake of the lands they held in England. It was probable that some at least would change sides when Curthose came home, as they also held them in Normandy.

Henry knew who they were; two knelt early before him, and the king surveyed the bent necks with irony; one belonged to Robert de Bellême, whose blood led him to abominable unseen, but rumoured, deeds, and whose mother Mabel, a poisoner, had been murdered in gruesome fashion in the Conqueror's reign, to the relief of most. The other was Hugh of Chester, a moody man who might do one thing or the other. Meantime, friends such as Robert FitzHamon and old lame Simon de St Liz of Northampton, and the de Meulan clan, rallied round to sign charters and lend strength.

Henry's other certainty was that he must establish firm relations with the church. Rufus had made the mistake of keeping the money which accrued from vacant benefices on the deaths of bishops without naming successors, and had generally abused the establishment except once, when he fell ill at Gloucester and feared he would die. Henry himself knew he would keep the appearance of submission, while exerting himself to establish his mastery as regarded making bishops of his own.

Meantime, he must secure the approval of the archbishop of Canterbury, the saintly but stubborn Anselm, who had been driven abroad by what proved an irreconcilable quarrel with Rufus, and must be caused to return to ensure the legality of his, Henry's, marriage in the event. He sent off prompt letters to the primate, who was still at Bec, urging him to return. Henry then arrested the bishop of Durham, a man of common origin and known vices, a crony of Rufus named Ranulf Flambard, and clapped him in the Tower. That done, Henry arranged to have himself crowned again in several places later, in full view of the people; there must be no doubt in anyone's mind that he and no other was England's king.

The news of King William's death came to Wilton convent on an evening they were eating fresh carp from the ponds; on the whole, the food provided here was palatable and there was seldom need for stockfish. One of the younger nuns had been given the task of picking out fish-bones from the portion given to the ancient abbess, who mumbled, toothless and half blind, from her place at mid-table. It was said that she was old enough to remember, if she remembered anything, the reign of King Harthacnut, but nobody dared ask. Messengers came, and whispered to the Lady Christina, who murmured briefly to her superior and then rose, signalling for silence; there had not in fact been much talk allowed, and the young noblewomen who were sent here for an education sat sullen and inactive as usual, waiting to be served with their fish.

'There is news from Winchester,' Christina Atheling began in her harsh voice. 'The king is dead. He was slain by accident in the New Forest by an arrow while hunting. It is thought the arrow glanced off an oak, having been fired at a stag by his companion, the knight Tirel of Poix.' She ended with instructions to pray for

King William's soul, although admitting he had not been in good odour with the church.

Eadgyth felt tears of pity rise and roll down her cheeks. Nobody seemed to care one way or the other about the death of the king. There was a murmur that his brother Robert would succeed him, then that his younger brother Henry already had. She remembered only the red-faced man who had wordlessly asked for her help, and would have received it; now, it was too late.

She rose with the rest, and went later to the rich silver shrine of the young saint, kneeling there for a long time. Perhaps St Edith of Wilton, being half royal herself, would welcome the soul of the departed king and see it safe through purgatory. Eadgyth Matilda prayed that this might happen quickly. More she could not now do for the dead man.

Two days later her aunt sent for her again, not this time for punishment. It appeared that Prince Henry had not only seized the crown, but had sent word that he desired to marry her. Christina made no comment meantime: the matter must of course be discouraged.

The Lady Christina in fact hid an unmentionable secret, which partly accounted for her harshness towards her niece Eadgyth on entertaining possible thoughts of marriage with the late king or anyone else. She herself, her sister Margaret and her brother Edgar Atheling had been born in Hungary, where their father and his younger brother had been taken as children on the death of Edmund Ironside, their own father and, briefly, king of half England by right of descent. Both Ironside's sons had grown up and had married in Hungary, but the younger, another Edmund, died: at least, Christina supposed he was the younger; it was all a very long time ago.

Ambassadors had come from England at last, to say King

Edward the Confessor had no heir and to ask Christina's father, Edward the Stranger, to come to claim his inheritance. At first he had refused, though his mother Aldgyth had taught him to speak English; he was happy enough at the Hungarian court. When a second party of envoys arrived, however, the stranger had a son by his wife Agatha as well as two daughters. It was thought that for the infant Edgar's sake they should all set sail.

They had done so, and Christina could remember a farewell to the jewelled and incensed court of St Stephen, with its close kinship to the Holy Roman Emperor, the warmth of its furs and embroidered silks, the wild ponies one rode on the great endless plains. By now, she hadn't ridden for years; they had travelled from Romsey to Wilton by covered ox-cart, as befitted a nun.

Christina had decided to take the veil on hearing her mother Agatha's deathbed confession. It had revealed a deception which might have been more serious than it was by far, and have led to war; Christina's solemn mind took such things literally.

Their father, Edward the Stranger, on arrival in England, had been mysteriously prevented from seeing the Confessor. The reason was made shamefully evident now. Princess Agatha, their mother, was not, as had been supposed by everyone, a daughter of King Stephen after all – that had been Edmund's wife – but of the bishop of Augsburg, and that at a time when priests' wives, as a result of the decision from Rome regarding celibacy, were being sold into slavery in Germany and elsewhere, though it had not yet happened in England. Someone, possibly the sly Archbishop Stigand, who favoured William of Normandy as next king, had passed the information to the holy Confessor, who had expressed his horror and had refused even to set eyes on the newly arrived heir from Hungary, though he and his wife continued to be kind to the children. Edward the Stranger had chanced to die then, not having been long on English soil. Christina, Margaret and little

Edgar had been brought up piously at Westminster by the king and his Lady, Eadgyth Godwinson. Then there had come the death of the Confessor, the election of the Lady's brother Harold by the Witan, news of the Norman fleet setting sail, the battle at Hastings, and confusion and fear at Winchester, whither the Lady herself had fled. However the Conqueror had treated her in friendly and respectful fashion and had permitted her to depart to her estates. One of these was in the south and the other in the north of England, and in the latter Eadgyth Godwinson greatly preferred to reside. Christina herself had visited her there, on her own way south after the quarrel with King Malcolm over the matter of the nun's veil she had briefly placed on young Eadgyth's head at Dunfermline. There had been, she recalled, a witness there, the duke of Brittany, who tiresomely also wanted to marry young Eadgyth Matilda himself. The girl's mother, informed of everything, had agreed with Christina that it was best that none of her children should marry at all: there might be scandal if the ancestry was discovered. They must certainly become monks and nuns.

Christina scowled. She and Margaret, when they were both young, had sworn to take the veil together, but the storm had intervened and it had been impossible to stem the ardour of King Malcolm when unexpectedly encountered in Lothian. Informed, he had taken Margaret by the shoulders and had said 'Woman, I am not marrying your grandsire, but yourself,' which had settled the matter; and after that six boys and two girls of the marriage followed. One of the former, Edgar, reigned in the north now, the usurper having been brought down, but had obediently not married; neither had Ethelred, who was a lay abbot, nor Edmund, who after his betrayal to the usurping rival, Donald Bán, had become a monk and had asked to be buried in chains as a penance to be observed when they all rose again on the Day of Judgement. Young Edward, of course, had been killed alongside his father, or shortly after. It was impossible to foresee what Alexander and the even younger David would do; but the two girls were, or had been, under Christina's control, and must become brides of Christ.

Well, worldly things were after all unimportant. That had been made evident in the visit Christina had paid, in her long-ago passing, to the late king Edward's widow, who it was said had never been a wife. The Lady Eadgyth Godwinson lived now for the most part not far from Stamford Bridge, the great battle caused to be almost forgotten by that at Hastings, which had followed immediately after the long march south by King Harold's men. At Stamford Bridge, Harold had fought and killed his own and the Lady Eadgyth's favourite brother, Tostig, who had once ruled Northumbria. She spent her time up here praying for both their souls and for her other brothers, Godwin's sons who had died at Hastings alongside their brother Harold and Sweyn, who had also died on his pilgrimage to Jerusalem following rape of an abbess. There was a great lake beside which the former Lady of England would walk daily by then, telling her beads; she had the remains of beauty, which had never moved King Edward, and had long adopted the habit and the ways of a nun. Inside the hall, there was one more reminder of the old Saxon times in England; a very ancient woman, withered like a leaf, who sat hunched by a brazier of sea-coal, winter and summer, to warm her bones. She had once been golden Gytha, wife to Earl Godwin and mother of many sons, and the single daughter with whom she now passed her days. 'She is more than ninety years old, and her wits have gone long ago,' murmured the Lady Eadgyth. 'It is as well, as her last memories were sad.' Behind the old woman, rearing darkly, lay the great helm and sword of Earl Godwin of Wessex. They said he had been a Sussex churl's son. Gytha herself was kin by marriage to King Cnut, and all her children had had the golden hair of the north lands. Her own was grey and sparse now, covered by a cloth. Christina shuddered, and hoped she herself would not live to be as old; but in the cloister one often survived to a great age.

Thinking and remembering, she was approached by one of the lay sisters with word of great importance from London. The king was dead, and his brother Henry had been crowned as next king of England. Archbishop Anselm had been recalled from abroad, and desired speech with her shortly on a matter of great urgency.

Christina had sent for young Eadgyth and told her of the circumstances of Rufus's death. 'You may pray for his soul if you will,' she said coldly. 'He was buried next day, with a hunter's mass only, below Winchester tower, deep in earth as befitted the sinner he was.' She took no heed of the tears that rolled once more down Eadgyth's cheeks; but shortly other news came that alarmed her more greatly than that of William II's death. The new king, Henry, desired to marry Eadgyth Matilda himself. It would be difficult to gainsay Archbishop Anselm, or for that matter King Henry, now firmly crowned. She must put forward the argument that Eadgyth was already a nun.

She was gainsaid, and there was no disobeying the further orders of the archbishop of Canterbury that both princesses were to be sent to him at once. The Lady Christina sent for Eadgyth again and harangued her; the man who desired to marry her was doing so only because of her royal blood; he himself was a lecher, with bastards littering England, Normandy, France and perhaps Germany as well. 'You would be by far happier in the cloister. If you insist on this the archbishop will heed you. See him, then return here and take your vows. No one can force you thereafter to marry.'

'But you would force me to be a nun, aunt, and as I have said already I have no vocation.' She had turned white, then red, at the mention of Henry's bastards. It was evident, her aunt decided, that the prospect of freedom prevailed on her more than the thought of the bridegroom's habits. Christina looked at the set young mouth, saw the waiting litter outside, and knew she must, meantime at least, succumb. 'I can but pray for you,' she said angrily. She then watched the two, Eadgyth and Mary, collect their few belongings, saw these stowed safely in a box beneath the wheels, and watched the conveyance prepare to depart. A small crowd of persons of the kind who always sniff out pending events had gathered beyond the new stone buildings, having come from Salisbury. They stared at the slender girl who, they had heard, was to become their queen; then at her plump little sister, wondering who would be the latter's bridegroom. The two princesses climbed in and the litter swayed off. 'We are to go to Lambeth,' said Mary happily. She was flushed with excitement; to be out of Wilton at last! Eadgyth seemed quiet, Mary thought. Perhaps she didn't want to be married. 'Would you as soon have stayed?' the younger girl asked.

'No.' She knew as much as that, and that the future was, suddenly, unguessed at. She tried not to resent the fact that Henry had a number of children already. It wasn't the children's fault. She would be kind to them.

Anselm, for the past seven years to his grief archbishop of Canterbury, and for the past two absent by reason of exile from his see, was reflecting on his quarrels with the late King William and the possibility of similar disagreements with King Henry. For one thing, Henry wanted to re-invest him in office, and Anselm considered himself already invested; Henry also had already conveyed bishoprics in his, the primate's, absence, which act should by rights be contested by reference to Rome. Nevertheless the primate was not anxious for trouble. He had received news of Rufus's death at

Chaise-Dieu near Lyons, brought to him there twice over, once by a monk of Canterbury and likewise by a monk of Bec. At the latter place Anselm had been in his time for many years abbot, and had enjoyed good relations with its overlord, Fitzosbern, Proud Spirit of Hastings, who in the nature of things was loyal to the reigning duke of Normandy, Robert Curthose. Nevertheless Henry was by now crowned, though not by oneself in England, whereas Curthose, newly returned from Normandy, showed no haste to abandon the ease of living for which he was once again notorious, having meantime won great respect for his prowess in the Holy Land. It was one thing to have fought so valiantly that no man was said to be able to unseat him, and to have refused the very crown of Christendom; but now, Curthose stayed in bed in Rouen so late his servants were said to steal his clothes. It would require some urging to induce him to exert his rights to England, and perhaps result in a sickening war. Henry, on the other hand, seemed energetic and able, and had certainly written the news of his accession in a most clerkly hand one could read, a pleasant change from most documents. Altogether Anselm had decided to return, especially after hearing that the new king had already clapped the disgraceful bishop of Durham, Ranulf Flambard, who had been responsible for many of the late king's extortions, in the Tower.

Another factor was Henry's intended marriage. It would certainly heal the breach between Saxon and Norman if a descendant of the line of Alfred and the old kings could become Henry's queen as he evidently desired; but one must make certain, by questioning the young woman herself, that she had not, as was strongly rumoured, already taken conventual vows. That would make marriage out of the question. He himself must see to it, and later consult the bishops. He had acted swiftly after arrival, sending three holy women still in the world to take the princess Eadgyth Matilda out of the custody of her aunt at Wilton, to command the aunt to stay where she was, and to bring the princess and her sister to Lambeth. Anselm was riding there now, the fresh wind of autumn stirring his white hair: he was sixty-eight years of age, and had always found the pallium a burden; he would infinitely rather have led the existence of a hermit, but that had not been permitted. The same fate had overtaken the holy Lanfranc, the blessed Cuthbert, the blessed Alphège; the last had been pelted to death by the Danes with bones after feasting, early last century. Thankfully those days seemed over. He himself had persuaded the pope to let Alphège remain on the calendar of saints: his holiness had been assiduous in censorship, and had removed a great many long revered by the English.

Anselm scattered his own blessings among the crowds, who thronged to watch him pass; like Christ, he had compassion on them, although solitude was necessary to him when he could find it. Entering at last into the hall at Lambeth, he was told that the Scots princess was already here. He sent for her after he had refreshed himself. He was unaccustomed to address women directly and kept his eyes meantime on the ground. Her mother, Queen Margaret, he had heard, had been beautiful as well as pious. It remained to be seen how the daughter would conduct herself, now that she was free of constraint if indeed there had been no vows taken. There had been worse queens of England than she might make. He heard her enter.

'Greetings, my daughter.'

'Greetings also, and your blessing, I hope, my lord archbishop.'

Her voice pleased him greatly, and despite himself he looked up. She stood alone, dignified and slender in a plain long cloak, her gaze clear and direct, her fair skin flushing easily. He could perhaps perceive the ghost of the mother's fabled beauty in the fine high carving of the cheekbones. Margaret Atheling, he believed, had had long plaits of incomparable fair hair. He averted his thoughts from such things and began to question Eadgyth Matilda. She answered without hesitation; no, she had never taken vows; she had been made to wear the veil by her aunt, even with blows. Her aunt had put it on her from time to time even in Scotland, for her protection.

'Would you be prepared to swear as much before an assembly of bishops? Remember that God is not mocked.'

'I would never mock Him. I will tell the truth to my lords spiritual. I have never desired to be a nun.'

She swallowed, blushing deeply. 'There is one thing my aunt told me,' she said. 'King Henry has a number of children, although he has never been married. That troubles me a little.' She had continued in shock after Christina told her, spitefully, that the man she was to marry was a lecher.

The archbishop answered evenly. 'If you swear to love and honour your husband, he will love and honour you in return. You must remember that Henry's mother died when he was fifteen, and that like yourself an attempt was made to force him into the Church. After that he was at war with his brothers, an exile on the borders of France and Germany. He took such consolation as he could, and also to prove himself unsuitable for sacred office since the strict decrees of Pope Hildebrand.' Anselm stared down at his gleaming archbishop's ring; would this girl understand, did he himself understand, the turmoil which had greeted that fiat, that no priest henceforth should marry? He, Anselm, had never felt the lure of the flesh, being occupied with scholarship and prayer, at first against the opposition of his family, especially his mother. King Henry's life had been different. The marriage, as Anselm made himself explain to their descendant, was valuable to the people of England who remembered their old kings. That was her duty, to love her husband and bear children of the marriage, who would inherit his blood and hers. 'It is a high calling; I think you will be worthy of it,' he ended quietly. This girl had a gentle authority which would not fail her.

There were sounds of arrival without. 'Here is the king now, I think,' said Anselm. He had not yet told Eadgyth Matilda that she must lose her first baptismal name; it had been decided that Matilda by itself would be more suitable in a time when all things Saxon must be made lower in degree than most things Norman. Henry had pretended that the common people would not be able to pronounce Eadgyth, which was unlikely, remembering the Confessor's queen who had often gone among them: but there it was.

Henry came in, leading a well-grown boy of about fourteen. He came straight to Eadgyth Matilda, having knelt formally and briefly to the archbishop. 'This is my son Robert, who was born in Caen,' said the king. 'I know you will be kind to him.' He was smiling, not today wearing his crown; the long robe gave him dignity, and he had grown a Saxon beard, which became him.

Eadgyth found it impossible not to love young Robert; he had clear eyes and open features, and had been taught courtly manners. She kissed him, to everyone's approval. The presence of Henry did not now disturb her. She could understand that he must have been lonely, like herself.

Eadgyth Matilda acquitted herself well before the assembly of bishops. She had never seen as many assembled churchmen in her life, or as many men at all; but if one told the truth it was easy enough to know what to say, having prepared first, by personal prayer. She kept her glance fixed on Archbishop Anselm's gleaming ring, only occasionally raising her eyes to survey his wise face. He questioned her seldom after the first; had she ever taken conventual vows?

'Never. My father King Malcolm used to swear that no daughter of his would be a nun. I remember when he tore a veil in rage from my head when my aunt put it on me. If I ever wore it, it was for protection. I used to jump on it in private.' She saw them smile, and knew she had won them over. When she told them that her aunt had tried to force her with blows to take the vows, there was a shocked rustling among them; the low-set mitres converged like so many broad white leaves, conferring together in a breeze.

It was decided that the day she married the king, the archbishop himself should address the people first from a platform raised above the street outside King Edward's new abbey of Westminster. He would assure them once and for all that she was not, and had never been, a nun. She saw the bishops glance at her here and there, overcoming their habit of not looking at any woman if it could be avoided; like Anselm they saw a slender girl with high, gallant cheekbones and a clear direct gaze. She had answered without fear or evasion; she would make a worthy queen. One of them spoke up about the dying King Edward's prophecy; the tree that had been cut down should bring forth green shoots. He meant Eadgyth Matilda's great-grandfather, King Edmund Ironside, who had been killed by treachery among the invading armies of Cnut. Ironside had been the son of King Ethelred Unred, who was himself the son of Edgar the Peaceful, father, without benefit of clergy, of little St Edith of Wilton. Sooner or later all things became one.

She made her obeisance to my lords spiritual, and went back at last to where Mary waited, curious to know what had happened but asking nothing. 'There's wine,' said Mary practically. Eadgyth drank with gratitude, her mouth dry after speaking. She still could not believe that all this had happened. She would wake up in the cell at Wilton, and find that it had been a dream. Besides the wine, they had provided a jar of rosewater. Eadgyth rinsed her fingers in it, feeling them soften and grow fragrant. This was what it would be like to be a queen, partly at least: the rest was not yet certain.

'I will call you Mald,' said the king to her. 'It is the name my father used to my mother.' He did not mention the suppression of her name: it had been arranged, evidently, already.

It was already planned also that they should marry in early November, before Advent. Henry had thought of everything: the church disapproved of intercourse during both penitential seasons, and he was anxious for an heir.

The people of London accordingly streamed towards Westminster on the eleventh day of November, 1100, no longer either remembering the Confessor, who had built the new abbey there, or the late king dead only three months. They had a new interest, perhaps even a new loyalty; King Henry was today to marry the daughter, as had been proclaimed, of 'the good Queen Margaret, King Edward's kinswoman, of the right royal race of England.' She was no doubt a suitable bride for the prince who had always called himself their Atheling. Her father, King Malcolm, was mentioned in passing, but not stressed; they thought of him, if any did so at all, as a freebooter who now and again harried the north parts for reasons of which they remained stolidly unaware. The blessing was the renewal of the old royal blood in their own future princes. They were happy, ate roasted meats from the Thames cook-shop and waited for a sight of the bride. In the meantime, they were edified still further by the appearance of the great Archbishop Anselm himself, fully vested: he who when in Rome had been called, even there, the pope-from-over-the-sea, with the people crying to see him and to pay to kiss his feet. He had mounted a platform and was addressing them, saying that the Princess Matilda had convinced an assembly of bishops that she had not at any time taken conventual vows, and was therefore free to marry their king and become their queen. Everyone hoped that that meant certain issue, many of the older ones not having forgotten the strange marriage of the Confessor, which had understandably produced none. As for the last queen named Matilda, she had come to England briefly from abroad, had spent two years here with her husband, the terrible Conqueror – even at his coronation Westminster had burst into flames, destroying folks' houses – and had duly conceived and given birth to a prince in England, the bridegroom of today. They had already seen King Henry enter, pale, dark-haired and dignified in his long robes, wearing his crown and bearded lately as the old kings used to be. It looked like a return of happier times, although one never knew.

The bride arrived, having travelled from Lambeth by water. As she came up from the wharf there was a growing murmur of approval. She was young, slender, had modesty and dignity, and wore a crimson robe trimmed with white fur. It kept her warm, no doubt, against the November cold; they themselves were close-packed enough to warm one another, thinly clad or no. The good Queen Margaret was said in her day to have been charitable; maybe her daughter would do something of the kind for the poor. They strained to see her face, which some who contrived this said had flushed to the very colour of her robe; she passed into the abbey, followed by her sister and her women. Candles shone on the altar; having done with his speaking the archbishop descended, and followed them in, his mitre gleaming. It was said he was a very holy man; it was as well he had returned in the new reign, to keep certain things as they should be.

The vows were taken. Mald – she had tried to grow used to Henry's new name for her – felt the strange firm grasp of a man's hand under the silk cloth; she also felt Henry's ring slide on her finger, and put her own on his. They were instructed to love one another, and she was told to obey her husband. She was, after all, used to obedience; and Henry would certainly be less harsh than the Lady Christina.

'Now they will hallow you to queen,' he murmured. He was pleased with her appearance; she was a credit to him, as he had anticipated. He led her to where they anointed her, and placed on her head the small crown the Lady Eadgyth Godwinson had worn now and again on high occasions; his own mother's was in Normandy, where she had died. The crown itself was light; Mald did not feel it burdensome. She allowed her husband to lead her, hand raised high and borne, on his wrist, out of the abbey to the renewed acclaim of the people. The cry of 'Queen Matilda' still sounded strange; but she must cease to think of herself as Eadgyth at all. She had promised to love and obey, and she always kept her promises. She must become a new person, as her mother had become when she married after all, having never intended it.

One face absent from the wedding ceremony, and the later feasting, had been that of Mald's erstwhile suitor, the discomfited earl of Warren and Surrey. He had slipped away to rejoin the returned Robert Curthose in Normandy, expecting better fortune there.

After the feasting, still heady with wine, the royal couple were brought to the marriage-bed. They knelt, naked as Adam and Eve before the Fall, for the church's blessing, beside the four-poster with its fur covers turned down ready; but it was not cold in the chamber, being crammed full of people. Mald felt continuously that this was happening to someone else; she had never been seen naked before, and had never herself seen a naked man. The presence of Henry beside her was less strange than it had once been, but she glimpsed his member, the first she had ever observed in her life. At her mother's strict and gentle court of Dunfermline no such sight had been permitted openly, and certainly never at Romsey or Wilton. Even her own youngest brother David, when he was born, had been swathed and cradled before she herself set eyes on him. She closed her eyes and tried to accustom herself: other women had done so, after all.

The prayers were finished and she and Henry were alone. She remembered her sister Mary's soft parting kiss. Mary had been called after the Mother of God, a name owned by few. The Blessed Virgin herself had evaded this unknown experience which now awaited herself. Henry had doused the remaining candle, and she felt him approach her beneath the furs. She knew that she herself was not uncomely; her hair had been allowed to grow shoulder-length since the Lady Christina's last compulsory shearing. Nevertheless Henry's long locks soon covered them both where they lay. His beard was soft against her neck; he had begun to caress her slim breasts, a proceeding Mald found strange but pleasant. She began to tremble. 'Do not be afraid,' she heard him say.

The soft white hands travelled knowledgeably down her limbs. They were, he thought, like the pliant white stems of wood bluebells, readily crushed. He did not want to hurt her; but the slender body, still almost boyish, did not induce desire in him; he preferred large-breasted women, like young Robert's mother at Caen. He entered her, and began to feel, within himself, only a cold and deadly triumph. He was here, in Rufus's place, with Rufus's intended bride, if that had indeed been so. Rufus himself was rotting, forgotten, under Winchester tower. He, Henry, had overcome all opposition; but to awaken himself and his bride to a pleasure she was too innocent to know needed more, by far. He took thought, then withdrew for the time.

Mald had already begun to feel the onset of a shy delight. This must be the love in marriage her father and mother had felt. She put out a hand presently to stroke the beard Henry had probably grown to please her; but he had risen, and she saw him take a taper and go out.

The king had left the white chamber where they lay, and went into the further one. Figures of saints with haloes of beaten gold reared on the walls, monstrous in the moving, streaming flame. Further off, in the shadows, the great bed reared in which Edward the Confessor had died in the odour of sanctity. It had been used for nothing since; even his father had not ventured to sleep in it.

He lit other tapers, extinguished after the departing of the company; soon the room was warm from their assembled flames. He went back to his bride, wrapped her in the fur coverlet till only her white feet showed, and carried her past the brazier through the door-arch. She remained unquestioning, her eyes wide.

He laid her on the hallowed bed, and climbed upon her. An excitement was stirring in him which had not come earlier. Here the old fool of a king had lain alone, while Earl Godwin's golden-haired daughter remained virgin and could therefore bear her husband no heirs, the Confessor having maintained the vow of celibacy taken in youth at Jumièges.

Henry heard himself laugh inwardly. Celibacy! Had it not been for that, there would have been no Norman Conquest. He would make his own conquest here, in old Edward's bed. Presently he heard the sound of his own laughter.

'In my brother's day the men wore tight-lacing and curled their hair. In the days before that, saints didn't couple. We are coupling now, eh?' He felt the bed quiver, and his seed flood into her at last upon the gentle, initial sliding open of the finally attained womb. Old Edward had given his benison, or perhaps his curse; whichever it was, he himself had consummated his marriage. He must be careful of this bride, whom he knew to be devout; not letting her health be endangered either from excessive time spent on her knees, or penances in approaching Advent. By Lent, at this rate, there should be news of an heir.

He became aware of a strange babbling from her in a tongue he did not understand; she had gone, in the ecstasy, back to her childhood Gaelic. Curthose would have understood her; he had the gift of languages, but Curthose was not here, any more than the ghost of Rufus. Henry laughed again, stretching himself in her: then at last finished. 'Come, sweet, we must be found back in the same bed by them all in the morning.'

He carried her back, then returned to extinguish the tapers. On the whole, he was content with his marriage.

4

FOR SOME TIME Henry was pervaded by this feeling of domestic contentment which he had never before experienced. He was aware that certain of his courtiers, remembering the uproarious days of Rufus, sneered at the resulting change in court manners. He himself had forbidden the wearing of tight-lacing for men, and for them to curl their hair was no longer the way to royal favour. The days passed without further apparent change; now, there was mass, breaking of fast, council, the hunt, dinner and early bed; and in bed the king lay by habit with his wife. He took increasing pleasure less in Mald's body than her mind. He had never before encountered complete goodness, complete innocence, in a woman; even his mother, Matilda of Flanders, could be vengeful. This queen of his was forgiving, calm and pious; except that he could rouse her to a bodily response that almost made her forget her God. The fact pleased him greatly, but he also respected her and did not exploit matters.

He began to invite her to sign documents, to be present in council, take part in the talk he had daily with men he could trust, such as the de Meulans and FitzHamon. He could rely on Mald's judgement, he discovered, as greatly as on theirs. She had also begun, in the tradition of her mother, to do what she might for the poorer of his subjects. Henry was pleased by this also, although it meant spending money on her charitable doings, sending wine and meat and new clothing when old would have done as well. The common people already called her Good Queen Mald. He himself valued her also as his hostess, in particular to foreign guests who had begun to cross seas to visit Westminster. One of these was the King of France's heir, a fat young man named Louis. Mald talked to Prince Louis gently and made him feel at home. This was of importance; if France became an ally, it might well lead to better relations with Rome than had been the case in his brother's day. It did not matter that some of the latter's old drinking companions called him and his queen Godric and Godgifu, any Saxon couple. Henry was aware of it and of who they were, and bided his time.

He took the French prince hawking, with his company. The queen did not always accompany them; she said she pitied the harmless prey, brought down in its blood. Henry laughed; such notions were her own, he himself had a passion for the sport, like all his family. Nevertheless on a day when they rode down to a place formerly called Windleshore, because of the winding of the river, where he planned a new palace, he kept close by her side, talking about the furbishings needed there and in the old apartments in the tower, which had grown shabby since his father built it. Mald had her mother's taste for splendour, and could be trusted to render everything as it should be. The rascally bishop, Ranulf Flambard, was still held there; Henry remembered idly how Ralf's old mother was said to have lost an eye when she lay with the devil. Few could escape from his father's fortress, rearing white as it did above the Thames. It was strong, like Falaise in Normandy.

Down here, at what was now slurred by custom to Windsor, Henry intended to found a menagerie; he was fond of animals, and the close conditions of the lions kept in the Tower open cells displeased him; he would like them to have room to roam freely, and have lynxes peering bright-eyed from among the branches;

and Mald's eldest brother had already promised a camel from Scotland which had been brought back from the Holy Land, and no doubt felt the cold. There would be other things, apes; perhaps a strange animal called a porcupine, which had grey-black quills it erected in danger. Henry thought with pleasure of what Windsor might become in such ways, instead of the plain hunting-box Rufus had maintained there. They would visit that today, to see what state it was in before necessary levelling. He had gradually removed all traces of the late king's presence from Winchester and Westminster; Gloucester remained to be visited.

He smiled, pleased; even Rufus's dogs obeyed him now. There was one which the dead king had especially favoured, and which now followed him and Mald, loping alongside them as they left the main party with its hawks still hooded; they would ride off to open ground presently, to free them. Among them was Robert the king's young son, riding boldly, a falcon on his wrist of his father's gift.

'Do you not want to go with them?' Mald asked; she was always considerate of him. 'No,' Henry answered, and called the great dog as they slowed together at sight of the hunting-box, which looked small and shabby. 'Odo,' he called to the mastiff, snapping his fingers. It had been named, with one of Rufus's twists of humour, after the renegade bishop who had been the Conqueror's half-brother, and had rebelled early in Rufus's reign on behalf of Curthose as rightful king of England. Bishop Odo had repented in the end and had gone on the pilgrimage to the Holy Land along with Curthose himself. He had however died at Palermo before reaching the desired goal. Henry scowled. Robert Curthose's wife, got with much dowry on return from the pilgrimage, had lately borne him a son. Mald must do likewise.

'Why are you frowning?' she asked. He smiled again, and caressed the dog's soft muzzle.

'I was trying to remember the name of a certain Roman general,' he lied. 'These mastiffs were in the land when Caesar came to these shores. Their size and speed astonished the invaders so greatly they took some back to Italy. I believe they hunt with them there still.'

'The Roman roads have lasted as well,' she pointed out. They were, in fact, the only reliable means of travel remaining to anyone. Perhaps, when things had settled down, she could suggest to Henry that more might be built in the same way. It would encourage trade.

She saw his grey eyes scan her with pleasure; her cheeks glowed with the cold from the ride, and the close riding-hood she wore became her. She felt the curious sensation, as often when Henry was near her, that her knees were turning to water; it was the beginnings of bed-pleasure, as she knew, but this was not the proper time. She let the groom take her reins and walked alone into the hunting-box, hearing Henry give orders to the men before he followed. It was pleasant after all to be married, and free. Everywhere they went people cheered them, and made gifts of cheese or stored honey; later in the year there would be fruit, cherries and apples in season. She was glad to be out of the convent. A bridegroom was on the way now for young Mary, if she liked him on sight; he was the son of the celebrated count of Boulogne who had fought at Hastings, and had, Henry told her, been famous in his day for his handsome moustache. As well as being rich, this young count of Boulogne was a Knight of the Swan, like his uncles Godfrey and Baldwin, who had become kings of Jerusalem. Henry had told her that also, and the Swan legend. He was well informed about everything, even law. He had improved these in England greatly already, as she knew; although he said he would not promise to amend the forest laws, as Rufus had done, and then break his word. 'They must remain the hunting-ground of kings and princes, as it used to be in the great forests of Normandy. That is why my father planted the New Forest, to be able to ride there easily from Winchester.'

She remembered his deep voice saying it, and entered the half-dark of the hunting-box. The dog Odo followed, sniffing at reminders of its old master. Suddenly it began to whimper. Rufus' bed stood foursquare, its leather curtains stirring slightly at the opening of the door. She went to it, and made the sign of the cross against the wooden post. There was a wreath of mistletoe hanging, brown and dry, from the upper frame. Mald felt herself afflicted with a feeling of dread, for no reason. She closed her eyes for instants, and heard the king follow.

'Why did you make the sign of the cross?' he asked jealously. 'He was ungodly; it meant nothing to him.'

'I think of him often,' she said, 'and pray that his soul may find rest. You know he came to Romsey, I think to offer for me; but my aunt prevented it.'

He was angry. 'Am not I good enough for you?'

She did not answer. On the bed was spread a great bull's hide, on which the hunter's tough body had been wont to fling itself down, no doubt with a minion. Henry jerked the mistletoe wreath from its place and sent the berries scattering, discoloured pearls by now, on the straw. He took her by the wrist, drawing her to the bed. It would complete his triumph to take her here, where Rufus had lain; he had after all done so in the Confessor's bed, and since then there had been ease between them in the matter. Yet she flushed deeply, then turned white as though she would faint. She swayed a little. 'Do not touch me now,' she said. 'It is broad day,' but he knew she still had Rufus in mind and not himself. He said a cruel thing, still coldly angry.

'You may not know that my brother William ordered the killing of your father King Malcolm by treachery, in the north. Morel of

Bamburgh was his creature and obeyed his order.' It was true; the old king had been stabbed by a man he thought to be his friend. She put out a hand then as though to ward him off.

'The women say I am with child,' she said unexpectedly. She had made no sign or gesture that she heard what he had said previously: it was as well. He kissed her, pleased at her news.

'You should have told me earlier, and not ridden out,' he said. 'Have a care from now on.'

He led her outside, thinking how his brother, in Normandy, would be checkmated if the child Mald bore should prove a son. It must do so. He asked her when the birth was expected; in early autumn, she said, at least she thought so. She had recovered somewhat as they emerged into daylight.

They would go, he decided, to Winchester for the birth. It was the old capital of King Alfred, and the arrival of his heir there would be fitting and would impress the people. They joined the returned hawking party, and rode home.

'Lady, will you grant this good woman a few minutes of your time? She is old and ill, and has come a long way.'

The king was absent, news having come of Robert of Normandy's invasion. Mald was herself heavy, though labour had not yet started; the child moved in her and seemed lively, though not due. The queen was in the lethargic state of mind of any woman with an unborn infant, and had even laid aside her task of sewing linen shifts for the poor. She waited, smiling gently, while the woman was brought in. She had been mindful of the value of this coming heir, and had spared herself in all ways; not fasting or tiring herself with penances, kneeling in church only when it was prescribed. Just now, she had been repeating the familiar prayers to the Mother of God, counting the mysteries with fingers grown white and smooth this past year with rosewater. Her robes were rich, though light today because it was summer; she had discovered in herself a liking for fine linen next the skin, splendour and rich shoulder-chains. The day was hot, however; it was almost a year since the late king's death. She remembered as usual to say a prayer for Rufus' soul; and with that, as though it had been planned, the old woman named Purkiss was ushered in. She had been brought by Edith de Monceux, evidently returned for the time from Normandy.

Edith's words that the old woman was ill were true enough; it was well seen the latter had not long to live. Her discoloured face was like lead, her breathing short and rasping. The queen stretched out a hand, as she always did to those in distress. 'In what way may I serve you?' she asked in her gentle voice.

The old woman had knelt with difficulty. She was not in rags, it having always been made possible for her to have a decent grey gown, shoes, though trodden over with use, and a hood which hid her grey hair. Her hands when she stretched them out were gnarled with ague and black beneath the nails; that was common enough. She spoke in Saxon, as most did outside the palace.

'My son is dead. I may safely tell you a thing he knew. While he lived, I dared not; the king that is now would have punished him.'

'Do not disturb the queen too long,' said Edith. 'Cannot you see the way it is with her? Tell your tale, and have done.'

The woman said then that it was her son's cart which had borne away the body of William Rufus. 'If he was dead, that is. Dead men do not bleed, and the blood dripped from him all the way to Winchester, and still while he lay in the streets here for all to see. That was why the king had him buried at once, next day.'

'These are ugly matters,' said Edith. 'Say what you came to say.' Her voice however held what might have been a kind of pleasure. Mald remembered that she was the sister of Earl Warren, now in Normandy with the duke. She made herself listen to the old woman's words. The latter had sat back on her bony knees, as though she began to feel at home.

'My son was found lying dead in the forest beside his fire two days since. I came straight to you, the good queen as they call you, with what he saw for himself a year ago. They may use me as they will; it matters nothing now. I will tell you, Lady. Prince Henry, that is king now, was standing behind a landmark oak, waiting. When the king came riding after a stag he shot at him, and he fell from the saddle. The other man made off. My son went to fetch his cart. He had seen, before that, the slaying of the duke's son, and the Saxon who shot at the old king's son earlier, long ago. The Saxon is a monk still. They cannot punish him. It was because of the folk who died when they made the clearings, and the many who died in the battle, that he did it. They do not want the Norman kings in England.'

'You are raving,' said Edith coldly. 'Come away.'

They led her away, grinning triumphantly and showing a few rotten teeth. Mald had whitened, and felt the blood in her body hasten towards the heavily filled womb. The child might well be born early with the shock of the news she had just heard; a murderer's child. Henry was his brother's killer, like Cain. He hadn't even waited to be sure the king was dead before they buried him. The blood had dripped on into the earth, deep down beneath the cathedral tower. William Rufus lay now in silence and darkness; a darkness she herself, after what she had just heard, desired. Perhaps she would die at this birth. The pains began.

She felt her woman Gunnhild's arms about her; the two had gone away who had come. 'Lady, I heard all of it,' Gunnhild said. 'True or false, do not lose the heir to England. That is what they want, for you to lose the heir. This heir to England is the people's hope, your child. You are greatly loved, Lady. The king is not, but he rules well, better than his brother. King Henry has made good laws. Think of that, and that many men have after all killed for what they desired greatly. Rest now, and wait for the child to come. It will not, maybe, be long to wait.' Her hands felt the younger woman's body with knowledge.

'Who brought her?' Mald heard herself ask. She could feel the rough linen of the waiting-woman's gown, rocking her presently as though she were a child herself. Her mother had held her so, long ago. She prayed to her mother's soul now, that she herself might do God's will; that she must after all love and not fear. A death, and a birth: a living birth, an heir.

'Lady, it was Earl Warren's sister who brought the old woman in, as you know, and Earl Warren's man who fetched them here, the old woman perched on his crupper. That lord himself may well be abroad, with the duke, for he gained nothing here from the king. He means if he can to destroy the king's child, and yourself; without you the king is nothing, any more than his brother the duke, who has a better right to the crown, though I shouldn't say it.'

That was Emma, who when she spoke did so out of turn. Gunnhild frowned, and silenced her. The queen remembered Warren faintly, with his talk of a right of his own to the crown, through his mother. It was all too much for her to remember, and she was suddenly tired and in pain. Gunnhild had begun a crooning, like the old songs of the makars. 'Live for England, Lady. Live for England, and the child they are waiting for to rule them as their chosen English king.'

Mald sat up, and put the woman away gently. 'I will remember what you have said,' she told them. 'I feel better now.' She managed to smile. 'You have saved your king, perhaps; but the birth will take place now a little early, I think.' There was a sharp pain jabbing in the small of her back. A king had been destroyed, the saffron-haired man who had once asked her wordlessly for help. A king should be born instead, and if possible should live.

*

After withdrawing from Pevensey, where he had expected to meet his invading brother the duke, Henry collected his thoughts on the way. All was not yet disaster; he had thought he knew Robert's mind, Pevensey being the place where their father had landed, fallen by mischance and bitten the earth; then had held it up in both fists to cheer his men and announced that he took possession of England. It was as if his father's spirit aided him now. His father had ruled with iron law; he, Henry, had so far done the same, codifying the laws both of Conqueror and Confessor. *A Lion of Justice shall arise in the land, making the lily like the aspen quake*. That was an old prophecy of Merlin's. If he himself was the Lion of Justice, as he believed, he would not be defeated now. He must use not weapons, but cunning, to achieve his aims; Curthose his brother must be persuaded to parley; he was affectionate and could be appealed to, despite the support of Warren and de Bellême. There was a place called Alton which might interrupt their line of march; Henry made towards it. For Winchester, and Mald, and their child, he said a prayer. No doubt news would come.

The queen lay in premature labour, while the town of Winchester was itself in turmoil which sounded in from the streets; many were carrying their goods away to try to bury them or else stack them in churches. Duke Robert's forces were advancing, it was rumoured; the king had not, after all, been in time. They were all of them in danger; this ancient place, the very key to England, was the first the invader would take; it had only been spared by the Conqueror because in their father's time the Confessor's widow had taken refuge here and had made terms with him.

Mald felt the continued warring in her body of a force she could not control. War or no war, invasion or none, this child would out; it was a strong child, caring nothing that her body was rent apart in its struggle to be free. The queen clenched her fists against the covers, also clenched her teeth; she must try not to cry out when there was so much distress everywhere. She had been in labour some hours when Gunnhild came.

'Good news, Lady. Duke Robert has passed by the town, saying he will not disturb your lying-in. He is a kindly man, they say. Easy, now: bear down, it's coming soon.'

Bear down. She had been at that now a long time; how much longer? How long was it since her marriage? Not nine months. She heard with thankfulness of the duke's consideration. He was her godfather. They had not met since she was an infant in arms, if then. Curthose was chivalrous, as Rufus had been; they said the late king had treated prisoners courteously. The late king. Henry had one brother left. He might show less mercy than Curthose himself had done earlier, on Mont St Michel, sending up water and wine when Henry made war. Henry. She was weary with long straining; she did not greatly care if she died.

She heard herself cry out suddenly, and the women come running. Something was emerging, a head. It was bald, being premature. It had struggled hard to be born into an unknown world. Perhaps death was like birth, coming out into the unknown.

They twisted it away. 'It's a fine little daughter, Lady. She'll come on. She'll grow her hair and her nails in time. What will you call her?'

Her first thought was of Henry's anger. It was all to do again; the English would not submit to a woman's rule. She watched them take the baby away to cleanse its mouth and nostrils. A fine little girl. She would call it Aaliz. It was a name that had occurred to her for no reason except that she liked it.

Before drifting off to sleep it occurred to her also that by avoiding Winchester, Robert Curthose might have lost himself England. Perhaps the brothers would meet somewhere, and give battle. There was nothing to be done but wait.

The rival armies met at Alton, and did not give battle, but instead parleyed for some days. As Henry had foreseen might happen, Robert Curthose fell with affection into his arms. 'You must be my guest,' the king told the duke, adding convivially, 'We will drink to my son when he is born. You kept him safe by avoiding Winchester.'

He felt doubly foolish when the tidings came that what was in fact already born was a daughter. However it gave Curthose an opportunity to boast of his own handsome heir, left at Rouen with his nurses. 'My wife,' he said, with sudden tears. 'My lovely wife. She's dead.'

Henry's feelings for his own wife were angry; why had Mald failed him? God had not. It would have completed his triumph to give England a prince at this moment. He led the willing Curthose to court, where the latter continued to drink deep, talking always of his lost Sybil, his wife and lovely girl. Earl Warren was present, sullenly. Robert de Bellême had, understandably, not accompanied them.

Mald, still in bed, stared at the fabled Curthose, who had come to salute her and the baby. The duke, whom no one could unseat from the saddle in any fight, whose courage in the East was unforgotten, round whose name legends gathered, who had refused the crown of Jerusalem after God had lit his taper in holy darkness three times, was no more than a little squat pot-bellied drunkard, red of face and unsteady on his feet. Fumes of wine were on his breath as he kissed her; but his eyes were those of a lost child. Like most others, she warmed to him.

'I am glad to meet your father's daughter,' he said. 'I remember King Malcolm well in the north. He was a fine man and a good king. His queen had given him a princess for the first time, yourself, after many princes. I gave you my mother's name, which you now use always.' Tears rose to his eyes. 'I loved my mother, and she loved me. She was short, as I am, while my father was tall. They loved one another. There were ten of us, but some never met the rest between England and Normandy, and Constance dead long ago of childbirth in Brittany, and Gundreda here in the north parts. I'm glad, my dear, that you survived your own labour.' It was a speech nobody but a man could have made, and she could not forbear smiling. Curthose however was already doleful again, remembering his lost wife.

'We called our son William after the bishop of Bonne-Ame, not for my father,' he said defensively. 'I unhorsed the Conqueror, I recall, when we were at war early on, he and I. As soon as I knew who it was I lifted him up; but he was gross by then. It's in the family. Henry will turn out the same in ten years, not a doubt of it.'

'Well, you and he are friends again. That is good news,' said the queen tactfully. Henry had come in earlier, kissed her briefly, stared down at the baby coldly, then had gone away. Later, she would say to him what must be said; but not now. She had schooled herself, as though she were still at Wilton, an intended nun according to the Lady Christina: perhaps that would have been better.

Henry bided his time, and on one occasion mentioned the lack of rule evident in the Norman duchy. Curthose gazed down into his wine.

'The law is a cruel thing,' he remarked. 'Did you know, brother, that in early days, long after old Rollo the Patrician hung his gold armlet on a tree for a year swearing he would hang any man who took it, there was a meeting of peasants to decide their rights? They sent delegates, one from each town, to the duke by then; it was past Rollo's time, as I say, and past his son's. The delegates had their hands and feet cut off, and were made to crawl home. Later on, in Richard the Good's time, there was a law made; any poor man who had his iron tools stolen could receive money from the duke. A woman stole her husband's harrow and some other thing, and the husband went to the duke for the money. Then she showed him where the tools were hidden, and being an honest man he went back to the duke to return the money. The duke kept him talking, and meantime sent men to pluck the woman's eyes out of her head. When the man got home, she was lamenting, and he said to her that she deserved her punishment and must henceforth obey the duke's laws. What do you think of all of that, you who are a law-giver?'

'Why, the delegates would be able to breed sons to dig the earth for them, and the eyeless woman could still knead her dough, while others would not dare to imitate her. Punishment fits the crime. If there was more of it in your dominions there would be better order. As it is, your barons do as they will.' There would be tortures among the poor, he knew, that their duke knew nothing of; Robert of Bellême alone was famous for the atrocious cruelties taking place in his dungeons.

'I am a merciful man,' said Curthose, weeping into his cups. The king decided that it would not be long before Normandy was his.

5

CURTHOSE STAYED ON with them into October, unwilling to return to an empty castle in Rouen which lacked its former lovely and welcoming presence. The child, of which he was proud, could not yet be a companion to him. 'There's nobody left,' he would say, seated with his short legs stretched out from a folding chair by Mald's bed, his sad gaze brooding always into a stoup of wine. He drank immoderately, and in that state was easy to persuade to anything. The king, before the court moved back to Windsor and then Norwich, got his brother to agree to exile the saintly Anselm once again if the latter would not conform to Henry's will. Anselm remained, defeated, in Canterbury, with eight years left to live. Little by little, Henry was consolidating his own position with regard to church and pope; the existence of a daughter to marry suitably would, after all, be a prop in the argument. He waited, watching at times while Robert showed how unfit he had ever been to govern Normandy; the dead young duchess had been better at it, and was much mourned.

'My lovely Sybil, my lovely dead wise girl. They say it was the midwife's fault; others say it was that damned widow of Giffard's, who hopes I'll marry her. I will never marry again, I tell you. We made our son together, Sybil and I, on Mont St Michel, your high rock, brother, the time we went there to give thanks for a safe return. There's an altar to Our Lady there, deep down; you remember it, I daresay.'

Henry remembered, and also recalled Curthose's gift of water and wine when he thirsted there; but he hardened his mind. The earl of Warren and Surrey kept close about him and the duke, having earlier followed the latter to his expected war. Warren could await the king's pleasure for the return of his lands; his old father had been given broad ones in England by the Conqueror after Hastings, they said enough to be covered by three days' hard riding; and the first William de Warenne must have ridden hard indeed. Henry prevented Warren's access to the queen, who might plead for him; Mald seemed in some way remote from himself since the baby's birth, possibly an effect on women after labour; he took little time to think of it, being engaged with finishing the Norman business and that of the recalcitrant old Archbishop Anselm, whom a convocation of nobles had already bidden obey the king or quit the realm.

The queen herself, after her churching at Winchester, knelt on there for some time alone, having dismissed the women and the court. Before her eyes, in the summer half-dark, many candles gleamed; but none for Rufus, though it was only a year since his death. Behind her was his deep grave, unmarked still. Did anyone pray for him except herself? Had he perhaps known, before the flight of Tirel of Poix, that it was his brother's shaft that had pierced his heart in the forest? Perhaps he would have chosen no other place to die; he had loved the hunt, and the old gods one must not think of here. She returned her mind to the tombs raised in front, those of Emma of Normandy, the Confessor's mother, through whom the Norman claim to England had come, and her second husband Cnut, whom she had loved. The first, King Ethelred, she had not, or her elder son by him, later the Confessor. Was it possible to dislike one's child? She, Mald, had no such feeling for her own little daughter as her mother in Scotland had had for herself. She remembered being told loving stories of Queen Margaret's own childhood at the court of the saintly king of Hungary, then later on the saintly king of England; and being taken to visit the Old Lady, as they called the Confessor's mother here in Winchester, when she had died. Emma of Normandy had however lived to a great age. Such encounters, such memories, were like a strand of gold between one generation and the next. She should no doubt garner tales of her own to tell her daughter; but could not.

She prayed on, the Good Queen Mald. She asked for strength and guidance concerning her husband. Had she the hardihood to remain silent over his killing of his brother? She knew that she must let him lie with her again, to conceive a son. It was her duty; but she had vowed to love and honour a man in whom was neither honour nor love. She herself was a vessel, no more. If she could have asked counsel of the saintly archbishop he would have spoken wisely in some way: but God could speak wisely also. Here, in this place, she felt that she was heard, was being told what to do.

'Bear your son, then love your poor. That is your task, to foster the common folk of England, those who have no hope but in you.' She remembered the Confessor's rumoured prophecy as he lay dying; that the tree which had been cut down would bring forth green shoots. She herself was of the blood of King Edmund Ironside, of King Edgar the Peaceful, of King Alfred the Great. She was the daughter of her mother Margaret Atheling, famed for her charities and piety, and of a line of northern kings who went back into the mists. She would not betray her lineage, her cause: God's reason why she had been born.

She rose from her knees at last, and left the place, comforted.

Henry had plans for Normandy. Evidently the duchy had begun to dissolve in chaos almost worse than that with which their father had had to contend in his boyhood. Curthose would never in nature rule firmly. After obtaining his assent to a state of affairs where Anselm would agree to consecrate those bishops Henry himself had invested, the king saw his remaining brother off, the latter murmuring bibulously that there should be no further exchanges between them other than hounds, hawks and jewels. When the ship had made away, Henry turned back to shore.

That night he was already making plans for a future Norman invasion. He had taken the opportunity at Alton to sound those who had followed Curthose to England, and had won many over. 'All will be yours in time,' the Conqueror had said on his deathbed, ironically watching the weighing out of Henry's allotted silver marks. Now, he possessed Rufus's legacy also: and Curthose would never again be persuaded to attempt England with an army. The king tried to plan where best to land in Normandy: it must happen next year now, or the year after. He must leave a son behind him, but Mald was not yet strong enough to bear a second child. Henry reached his hand down to caress the great dog Odo, who slept by custom beside his bed. In the darkness he felt its ribs unexpectedly stiff and cold. A dog died silently, after all.

Henry lit a taper, and surveyed the great fawn dark-muzzled body stretched on the straw. They had been companions often, and before that Rufus had kept the dog always by his side. No doubt its ghost had fled now to its former master. The king found his bedgown, and went to seek comfort from his wife. He had not visited her since the birth.

He called to a servant to take the dog's body away, and groped his way to Mald's chamber. He was shocked to find her on her knees, not yet disrobed, praying like a nun, a grey cloak cast over her head and shoulders. It was past midnight, and cold in the chamber. 'Why are you not abed?' he asked harshly. 'You should guard your health.'

She raised her clear gaze to him; he was suddenly filled with a discomfort he could not understand. Was it possible that his enemies had told her a certain thing, the truth about his brother's death? Yet it could not be so; there had been no witnesses, he had been prudent.

She spoke now. 'I will guard it enough to do my duty by you,' she told him. 'My duty, as I know, is to bear you a son. That I will do, if God sends me a child again; but I must tell you there will be no pleasure between us in the making of it. I know certain things of which I will not speak, now or later. After you have your son of me, I should like to take the vow of chastity my aunt would have had me take, and to live as a votaress, in penance and good works. You know why, my husband.' She had not taken her eyes from his face. He began to bluster, hearing his own voice over-loud in the chamber.

'You are crazed after labour. Women take these fancies. I will have my son of you, pleasure or no, as you will; that last I can find elsewhere.' It was a brutal speech and he knew it. She had not moved.

'As you will, also,' she said. 'I have told you that which I know, but I will tell no other man. The witness to it is dead; you cannot punish him.' She did not mention the old Purkiss woman; she herself might well be dead by now, she had not had long to live.

Henry felt his mind lighten; if the only witness was dead, he had the situation in his power. 'You are crazed, as I say,' he told her. 'I will leave you for the time. Go to bed, and warm yourself; you have prayed long enough.'

She rose, the folds of the grey cloak falling about her; for moments, she looked like a statue carved in stone. 'There will never be enough prayer for you or for me,' she replied quietly, then turned away and obeyed him, taking the cloak from her head and sliding her revealed white body under the bedcovers. She had cropped her hair. He had already turned and left her. On return to his own place he found they had taken Odo's body away. He had forgotten to mention the dog's death to Mald. The whole business disturbed him, and he did not sleep till dawn. Rufus, rotting in his grave, should be forgotten now by everyone; but was nevertheless remembered by his, Henry's, wife. Had the dog witnessed the murder? He had forgotten that also. In future, he must forget nothing in his ambition to master England and Normandy, must have compassion on no one in the achieving of it, the final and determined ownership of all his father's possessions.

That odd personage, Edgar the Atheling, had decided to go off by himself on pilgrimage to the Holy Land after everyone else who intended to do so had come home. Among those who did not were the elected kings of Jerusalem, said to be descended from the swan who had appeared to their grandmother, Countess Ida of Boulogne. The swan had turned into a shining knight who desired to marry her daughter. Godfrey of Boulogne made a modest king of the new Christian kingdom, his brother Baldwin succeeding shortly as Godfrey had no sons. At home, their young kinsman Eustace was duly betrothed to Mald's sister Mary. Now that Mald's companionship was to be lost to a happy marriage, Mald ceased to contemplate her own, and turned her attention more than ever to the poor and needy. She saw her brothers at times, though not Edgar who still ruled as king in Lothian, and whom she hardly now remembered; the last she had seen of him was when he helped to carry their mother's dead body out of Edinburgh in the providential mist that had come down.

David was here at court, grown to be almost a young man now; he was a quiet and prudent person who spent much time alone. He liked Henry, however, and was often to be found in his company, taking an interest in the way the king governed. It was as though

David expected one day to be a king himself: but there were elder brothers before him.

Edgar had remained unmarried, and two more were churchmen; Mald herself did not know whether Edmund, the repentant monk, was alive or dead by now, in chains as he had asked, in Somerset. There remained Alexander, who although he was known as The Fierce in the north – he had once chased a party of rebels across a river in high flood – was in fact a man of calm nature, like their father, and had their mother's love for beautiful things which Mald herself shared.

Alexander had ridden quietly alongside the Holy Land pilgrimage, taking the cross, and had returned with splendid Arab horses, a camel, silver trappings and a suit of Turkish armour; they had seen him, and them, briefly as he rode back to the north. He aided his brother Edgar in the further parts, by an arrangement made between them, and in return expected to inherit Lothian when Edgar died, but that might not in nature be for some time.

Meanwhile Alexander rode down now and again, and like David was much about the king. He was present at Mary's wedding, and saw her sail off to Boulogne with her gentle and devout Count Eustace. Next year, news came that Mary had given birth to a daughter, named Matilda after the queen her sister.

The Christmas season passed, with little Aaliz learning to walk; she was a solemn child, who already knew her own importance. On Twelfth-night Henry, flown with wine and expansive, came and lay with the queen. Mald endured it, recalling that her confessor had told her she must submit to her husband's rights while praying for his wrongs, which she had not unduly specified. She tried to do this, but Henry talked loudly meantime of the prophecy of Merlin's he applied to himself. *A Lion of Justice shall arise in the land, and cause the lily to quake like the aspen.* There was more of it, and she remembered the French prince Louis at court in the first year of their marriage; he had been friendly, there seemed no need to cause him to quake. Henry had certainly begun to codify a number of laws. However she remained silent, and a few weeks later found herself pregnant. She said nothing, as she wanted to ride to Canterbury in Lent to do penance at the tomb of St Alphège there, the archbishop who had been murdered by the Danes one Easter in the time of the Confessor's father, King Ethelred. It was cold by the time she set out, with a few retainers and without her women. The candles burned brightly at the tomb, Mald talked with Archbishop Anselm, frail now but writing his marvellous reflective prayers still; he cheered her, and she rode back with a memory of the rebuilt cathedral, smaller than it had been before the burning in King Ethelred's time, but still rising finely in stone. Preparing to cross over the old ford at the Lea she saw the river swollen high with rain; it had begun to blow, unnoticed by her, in their faces.

'Rest overnight, Lady,' said Rimbauld, her chamberlain; but she would not, and plunged her horse into the icy stream, taken up with thoughts of Canterbury, the comfort that had come to her there, and the need to avoid too much thought of heat and cold, or comfort of other kinds. As a result her horse slipped and she fell from the saddle, and felt the high stream carrying her away. Rimbauld waded in and caught her in his arms, and carried her, dripping and chilled, to the bank; but later Mald felt cramps come, and knew she had lost the child. She wept; the king came, and was angry that she had not told him of it.

'You had no right to ride to Canterbury, or elsewhere; your duty, as I have often told you, is to bear me a son. Now all is to be done again.' He saw her white face, and had compassion. 'Have a care to your health,' he said again. 'Do no more penances.' He went out then, no doubt to his concubines; they and their children lived in houses surrounding the palace. Mald turned her head aside and tried to sleep. One day, she thought, she'd build a bridge over that river at Bow. It must often be a danger to travellers, calm as it looked on most days.

Henry was occupied that summer with the rebellion of Robert of Bellême, who at last fortified his new castle of Bridgnorth against him. It was said to be the strongest ever built in England, and impossible to take. In the end, Henry took it after much fighting, despite de Bellême's knowledge of ballistics and sustained, calculated war. There were few nobles and institutions which held out by now against the king except, in some manner, his wife. De Bellême meantime made his escape to Normandy.

It was to be June of 1103 before Henry was able to send the bishop-elect Warelwast to Rome, with word for the pope that there was a fine prince born in England who would be called William, after Henry's father, the Conqueror.

Shortly before that, and having seen Curthose and his following off in the autumn after Alton, the king at least pretended to be much angered when word came that his brother was back, privately and without permission, in England. Had the earlier bribes and persuasion been for nothing? But it appeared that Earl Warren was the real cause, having persuaded Curthose to come with him to beg for the return of his, Warren's, English estates. Both men knelt at Henry's feet. It was undignified of Curthose; but the present duke of Normandy seldom showed dignity out of the saddle.

'Brother, I would ask for clemency for my good friend and follower Earl Warren and Surrey. He has lost all he owned in England through loyalty to myself. Now that peace is made between us, I have come in person with him in order that it may be seen that he will remain your loyal man.' The speech had quite evidently been suggested to him. Warren kept his eyes cast down. The king remembered the taunts of Deerfoot, long ago; and the presumption of Warren himself in considering Eadgyth Matilda, even briefly, for a wife. He turned over in his mind a way in which he could turn the visit to advantage. He said aloud, magnanimously, 'Loyal men cost silver. To return these lands and honours, under your oath I must have recompense. You have made peace in Normandy lately with Robert of Bellême, my erstwhile enemy, and there are church matters also.'

He kept Warren kneeling submissively, but raised Robert Curthose to his feet and said he would take him shortly to the queen. He had no hesitation in using Mald in the matter. It had been soon before the Audelin's birth.

He brought the duke and Warren to where she was. She wore her rich robes, but could no longer disguise the child in her, which sat well forward. Henry caressed her pregnant body openly. 'As you can see, I will have need of money,' he said, smiling; aware of Warren's discomfiture at the sight of his hoped-for bride big with another man's clearly begotten fruit, and that man himself, the king. He bent over Mald and whispered 'Do as I bid you. Do not be alarmed,' and then said aloud 'If I return these lands and honours to you, Earl Warren, you must become my loyal man and no longer go to war against me for any other master.'

'He has sworn it,' put in Curthose eagerly. 'He will reside in England. He will be as often at your side as Leicester and Warwick are.' It was known that the de Meulan brothers seldom left the king's company and advised him in all he did on either side of the Channel. Henry smiled.

'That will be rewarding. There is another form of reward. The late agreement at Alton gave you, my brother Robert of

Normandy, an agreed payment of 3,000 marks yearly at the conclusion of our war. If you will forgo this at the request of the queen here, your goddaughter, I will reward Warren and will take him into favour, and will arrange a marriage for him.' He was thinking of one of his many illegitimate daughters; he took an interest in them and wanted to see them married well now they were growing. Warren would serve, with his wide lands.

Curthose gaped; he was forever in need of money. The queen, heavy with child as she was, recalled her Gaelic; would her godfather, so briefly in the north parts long ago, but said to be apt with tongues, remember any? '*Mathanas*,' she breathed, watching Curthose's face. The word meant forgiveness.

He was at once the chivalrous model of Jerusalem's fame. '*Aír diochuímne*,' he replied, and forgiveness and forgetting were in both their minds. The king was less unworldly; he leaned forward sharply, angry that he was unable to understand what had passed.

Robert Curthose, duke of Normandy, then resigned his yearly allowance without protest. Warren and Surrey duly regained his lands and honours. Nobody except Curthose was the loser. He was allowed to return home to Rouen then, as if it was a favour. Bewildered, he recalled that, far from welcoming him, Henry had threatened to put him in prison as the invading ruler of another country who had entered England without permission. He remembered vaguely the rebellion led after his father's death by the late Bishop Odo, his old companion and half-uncle dead six years since in Palermo; and of how all of that had been on his own behalf as England's rightful king. 'By God's angels, had I been in Alexandria, the English would have waited for me!' he had boasted then. They had not; William Rufus had ruled in his stead, and there was no doubt who ruled England now.

Curthose sought the glance of his dead wife's brother, who had come with him and was as a rule his boon companion; but William of Conversano was of no aid today, being apt at dicing and drinking, no more. Their eyes did not meet.

Within Henry's mind was the certainty that Curthose could not rule in his duchy much longer; he himself had scattered bribes and persuasion here and there. He also evaded the gaze of the remembered childlike eyes. Robert Curthose, duke of Normandy, had begun to be aware, for the first time, that his brother Henry hated him. It was a state of things which his forgiving mind found hard to grasp. He had found himself unable to stem the tide rising against him in his own duchy. Sybil would have known what to do. Tears rose to his eyes at thought of her; she had been a pearl of a wife in their brief days together. Their son lived, thank God.

He returned, or was returned, home; and meantime in England the second earl of Warren and Surrey became King Henry's assiduous courtier, as if to atone for his past disloyalties.

In her own apartments, the queen gave birth safely to her son.

PART II

1

THE KING STOOD looking down, as he often made time to do, at the young William Audelin in his cradle. He was a fine strong baby, resembling Henry in feature, which fact gratified his father. The very adaptation of the Atheling's ancient title was a sign that all things and personages of high birth were henceforth to become Norman. Henry advanced his royal and clerkly finger; the child seized it in what was almost a manly grasp. The king smiled. After the birth he had gone to its mother and had said 'Now I have my prince, and you may have your freedom.' Since then he had visited other beds.

The small Aaliz was silent these days, and Henry guessed why; everyone was paying attention to her brother, whereas till now she herself had been of the first importance. They had even changed her name. He pinched her plump cheek. She was a handsome little girl; Mald had after all given him two fine children. Aaliz-Matilda would marry well in any case, being his daughter; but there was only one bridegroom of high enough degree, the one he had already chosen. 'Have no fear, sweetheart,' he murmured. 'You also shall wear a crown.'

One episode shortly after that left a bitter flavour. Alexander of Scots, the king's guest then, came into the hall one day to find his sister the queen washing and kissing poor men's feet. Some had leprosy, or what passed for it; none were comely. 'My sister, the king will not kiss you himself if he hears of this,' said Alexander idly; even their mother had not gone as far. Mald turned on him from where she knelt, her head bound with linen like a nun's beneath the netted gold caul. 'Fie, sir, did not Our Lord so? Take the chance yourself to do as he did.' But her brother only smiled, and went out. It was possible, he thought, to overdo such things; give the poor silver, it was all they asked: they would spend it on cheap wine, then go back to what they had been.

The queen had begun to distance herself in mind from her husband, though she was still often present in council by his invitation. Henry respected her judgement; and he knew she knew he went to other women; why not, as she denied herself to him? As for her, the remembrance of the pleasure her body had felt in the early days of their marriage had been controlled by harsh discipline. If urges for delight came upon her, she subdued them by prayer. It was her confessor's advice, though he had not been told the full underlying cause. Beneath her rich robes – they blamed her for a love of too much splendour – the queen wore horse-hair cloth next her skin, which thereby was scratched and lacerated. Once, the girl who had jumped on a nun's veil would have laughed at herself; but the queen by now had forgotten laughter. She was rewarded by the blessings of the people as she rode, saintly and dignified, abroad; here was the true descendant of their old kings, acting in a way they understood, a way very old folk remembered from the days of the Confessor. The king her husband they knew less well. He was engaged, had they guessed, in plans to seize Normandy; and was also in correspondence with the western emperor, who like his father Henry IV opposed the pope. It would be an assurance, Henry thought, that his own reign was accepted if what he had in mind came about; an imperial marriage for his young daughter, whose name he had determined to change to Matilda.

He thought of emperors. Curthose had met the eastern one in person in Constantinople; so in his day had their grandfather, Robert the Devil. The latter, refusing to stand in the sacred presence, had rolled up his cloak and discourteously sat down on the floor on it. On leaving, they had politely handed him the cloak. 'Normans do not carry their seating about with them,' the Devil had replied; his insolence was still remembered, but the present Emperor Alexius had received the pilgrims pleasantly when they came, and had sent them aid.

Nevertheless the western empire, begun with Charlemagne three centuries ago, was in conflict with the pope; this had come to a head when the present emperor's father, Henry IV, had had to kneel for four days in the snow at Canossa in the Alps, doing penance before the formidable Pope Hildebrand, Gregory VII, he who had forbidden priests to marry. The emperor, Henry's son, now Henry V, had betrayed his father and in the end, caused the latter's shameful death; it was said he had fits of deep remorse for it. Perhaps a wife would cure him. Henry watched his sturdy little Aaliz-Matilda grow, and planned her future. The emperor was almost forty years her senior; that was unimportant. The importance was that he and the German could become allies together against both France and Rome by such a marriage. France – young Louis had been a guest here early in course of one's own nuptials – was by tradition jealous of Normandy, the rich coastal strip unwittingly given away to one's seafaring pirate ancestors by Charles the Simple in exchange for peace. By now, Normandy rivalled France herself, and had ports; and he by now had yet more in England, and this recent alliance of young Mary's with Boulogne meant that trade was assured across the Channel for

English wool. The king narrowed his eyes and saw all such countries as a map, with their powerful rivers running towards the sea. It was perhaps not such a great loss that Mald had borne him a daughter.

That Aaliz must change her name Henry had early decided; the present one was not impressive enough for an empress. She should be Matilda, as his mother had been; as his queen had by now become even to herself. The Good Queen Mald had subdued her will to his, had behaved obediently, had borne the heir. He and she had no doubt contrived to forget what he was certain she knew. They could go their separate ways, and yet act in harness. He would entrust her with the care of England in his absence. More could not, after all, be said for any woman.

In the year after the Audelin's birth a boy baby had been brought to the queen, with a request from the mother that she rear it; she said it was the king's son. Looking down at its features, Mald saw that they were Henry's, but with an expression she could not help but love. She knew she loved also young Robert, the son the king had brought with him that time of their betrothal at Lambeth; Robert was much about the court, and young as he was had aided his father on several campaigns. The mother of this new child was a woman named Ansfrida, the widow of one Anskill, who had estates in Berkshire; the king had come upon her there, she said, when he renewed the lands to her after her husband's death.

Mald bade Gunnhild take the baby to the nursery, to be with her own son the prince; they were near of an age and could grow up together. When next she saw the king she told him of it, calmly.

'I have permitted you your vow of chastity,' Henry said. 'I myself took none.' He had in fact forgotten Ansfrida, and had an eye by now to the young de Meulan girl, Elizabeth; she promised to be as handsome as her brother Waleran and was not hunchbacked, like his twin Robert. At present young Bess Beaumont was being prudent, however, which spurred Henry on; prudence was in her father's family, though he suspected that the mother herself lacked it, being French.

'What would you that he is called?' he heard the queen say.

'What would you?' he replied courteously. 'You are to rear him.' He himself bred more daughters than sons, he was thinking; the marriages of some of the former would have to be arranged favourably, as he knew already.

'There were two young men both named Richard, who died in the New Forest from arrows. You already have a William in your heir.'

It was the nearest to a barbed retort that he would ever have from her. He answered easily 'That was the name of the old dukes of Normandy. Richard let it be.'

Richard grew, and being close about the Audelin always, was mistaken by many for a son of the queen's. Meantime Henry had thought of a bridegroom for his daughter Juliana, who was self-willed and needed a husband. He was anxious to secure the firm allegiance of Warren and Surrey, who retained lands in Normandy as well as in England; also Warren's brother Reginald adhered to Curthose abroad. The king wrote to Archbishop Anselm on the matter of such a marriage, which in his opinion should suit all of the parties concerned. Juliana's ambitions should be satisfied if she became countess of Warren and Surrey in England, and of the lands beyond the Channel in the Pas de Caux.

Anselm might be frail by now, but he was unafraid. He sent a letter to the king to point out that as the earl and the king's daughter were related in the fourth and sixth degrees of consanguinity, their souls would be in peril if they were to share a bed. Henry scowled when he received the missive; the old man had not forgotten

Gundreda, as he himself, her brother, had contrived to do. The long-ago relationship to the ancestress Duchess Gunnor, Duke Richard I's wife, with her many sisters who were forebears of almost all noble Norman houses including, by marriage, that of de Bellême, could be assumed and got over by agreed payment to Rome. This other could not, or not as easily; and mention of it would stir up reminders of Warren and Surrey's nearness to the throne. The king abandoned the notion, and as good fortune would have it found another husband for Juliana; his old enemy, William de Breteuil, the same who in the first place had pursued him to the treasury at Winchester and had attempted to claim it in the name of Curthose, died then, leaving no legitimate heirs. Henry married Juliana to de Breteuil's bastard son, Eustace, and saw the pair off to Normandy with relief.

Warren and Surrey appeared to take no umbrage, continuing his smooth self, promising once again to be the king's loyal servitor. He seemed much occupied with his castle of Lewes, with the Cluniac priory there his parents had founded, and with the markets and fairs in the town and the building of earthworks at Castle Acre in Yorkshire. No doubt he took women as he required them, like oneself.

Henry sailed for Barfleur in Lent, having sojourned a while with the court in Mald's old place of Romsey, but its memories had not brought them closer together. He had for so long by now sent spies into Robert's duchy, and was so well informed of what chanced there, that it was rumoured that he himself had come earlier in person to Normandy. Certain things pleased him; Tirel of Poix, who had been with Rufus on the fatal day in the New Forest, had, perhaps from fear, gone alone to the Holy Land and died there. That made one witness less; and strange tales were still being spread here about the nature of the late king's death. Rufus had been loved in Normandy, to which he had once come for aid to his subjects by jumping into the first unseaworthy boat there was, rather than delay. It was said now that the night before his death, he had had a dream of a stag lying dead before the altar, and that its blood made a fountain that spurted to heaven. That was the kind of thing, Henry thought, that the church would make of it; another tale, spread by his own agents, was that the stag had come between the king and Tirel, the king had shot at it but found his bow-string had broken; and he had called out to Tirel to shoot quickly, and the arrow had glanced off and pierced the king's heart. A third version was that it had struck a landmark oak and had then glanced off; but that tale was weak, the heart would not have been pierced. Nor had Rufus been found with a cut bowstring; it was Henry's own imagined tale of going to a cottage to repair a loose one that had taken a new form to itself, here across the Channel.

In fact there was more disaster than allowed for much consideration of Rufus's death. Robert of Bellême had made war here as he had done in England, with unspeakable punishments to those who fell into his hands; in the end Curthose had made a shameful peace with him, being upbraided for it by Henry on the late English visit. Also, there were the activities of Ranulf Flambard, the long-escaped bishop of Durham, who had installed two of his natural sons in church benefices at Lisieux and was living in greater comfort nearby than anyone else in the disturbed duchy. De Bellême had even burned down a convent of which his own sister was abbess; she and her nuns had taken refuge in a wood, but by now were in shelter. The poor folk were worse off by far, and many had perished in burned churches, while others had been left homeless after spreading fires; the king found this when he went into the church at Carentan on Easter Day. It was piled with tables, chests and beds, such goods as the folk had somehow rescued and stored; it was impossible to see the altar, and the bishop of Séez, who was expected to come to say mass before the king, entered ready vested, and stopped in anger. Henry sat quietly by the door near some baskets filled with chattels, waiting for what he knew would come: this was the churchman who had been unafraid when he pulled about the incorrupt St Cuthbert's remains at Durham, and he remained unafraid now.

'There is no room left to kneel before the divine majesty. Let the king arise, therefore, in God's name, and claim his father's inheritance with the sword of justice.' He compared Henry to King David, fighting not for grandeur but for his native soil. Henry examined his fingernails, remembering that he had won England as well by claiming that it was his birthplace; many English had come to support him here against the duke. He rose to his feet, aware of his own dignified appearance and the deep persuasive tone of his voice, which had never failed in council, and would not now in war.

'In the Lord's name I will rise to this labour,' he said, 'for the sake of peace, and with your aid that of the church.' Curthose had lately, it was rumoured, invested bishops with the staff and ring, a process resented in Rome.

He saw Robert of Leicester's prudent face approve; then beheld the archbishop, who was acting in a manner not foreseen. He had brought out a pair of shears. 'Offer an example to the sons of Belial, who for fashion's sake grow their hair long like women, and wear shoes like scorpions' tails, so that they appear both like women and like serpents,' said the old bishop piously, thinking no doubt of Lilith, the reviled first wife of Adam. He then seized the king's long hair and cut it off, audibly murmuring 'He-goats'. Leicester's hair and beard followed, and by the end a party of crop-headed, clean-shaven men in the manner of their ancestors emerged, having struggled meantime for precedence in being shorn. Henry knew he had grown the beard in the first place to please Mald, who was no longer pleased with anything; he felt the spring air cold on his shaven face, but cared little; the whole episode amused him.

He lingered at Carentan, where his lodgings were as comfortable as could be found in the time and place. The duke was said to have shut himself up in one of the strongholds he had managed to maintain. Henry thought of the hogsheads of gold and silver he himself had brought with him on the voyage out of England: it would serve to sweeten doubtful allegiance to another than *son droit seignor*, as the common people called Curthose; there was still enough affection left for him to have led to a cry for the heart of Robert FitzHamon, Henry's supporter, to be torn out of his body as he was borne prisoner lately through Bayeux. FitzHamon must be ransomed; he had been faithful ever since the unforgotten day of the hunting-party, five years ago now.

Henry frowned. There were knights-errant still among the supporters of Curthose. One was Warren's second brother Reginald, who had never wavered from the duke's support but was now Henry's own prisoner: another was old Edgar Atheling, whose presence in Normandy would not have been noted except for the king's assiduous spies. The Atheling must have returned from the Holy Land filled anew with tales of Curthose's remembered valour; he doubtless knew nothing of the genuine weakness of the latter's present rule.

Henry had not been deceived by treachery. Soon after his arrival he had received a peaceful message from Reginald de Warenne and others to ride, with only a few knights, to Dives for private talk. He had however taken seven hundred, had ridden all night, and had surprised the enemy at daybreak, taking them prisoner and setting fire to the monastery, whose abbot had himself been in the plot. Henry had had the holy man thrown like a sack across the saddle and brought to him in person, saying that but for his sacred orders he would have torn him limb from limb. In fact it was expedient to let him go into exile. Old Archbishop Anselm himself had travelled to his beloved Bec, and there would be the less blame from his ready tongue when the king duly heard it. A soft answer turned away wrath; the archbishop returned to England in the end, partly convinced by Henry that Henry's cause might, after all, be that of God.

Henry then attacked and set fire to Bayeux. Watching the flames rise and spread, the scurrying screaming people, he recalled old Biship Odo and his early rebellion on Curthose's behalf; his see had always been recalcitrant, the last centre for the ancient Viking pagans; their gods had lingered longer here than anywhere else in the duchy, being worshipped in a ring of wooden poles, burned now with the rest. Meantime the king was pleased to have back his released friend Robert FitzHamon, brought by the town's constable out of prison to try to placate the wrath of the English invader; but the flames burned high. Later on, in Caen, where his own parents lay buried, the people streamed out to meet Henry with gifts of money, fearing the same fate as Bayeux. Henry entered the town without bloodshed, which he always avoided where possible.

The first engagement came at Falaise, the stronghold of which town reared high above its river. It occurred to him, surveying the preparations for battle, that his father had been born here as a result of Robert the Devil's sighting of a tanner's daughter paddling in that same river. Of such small incidents great events followed.

The fight began, and Robert FitzHamon, by the king's side, was wounded in the head by a pike. It appeared that he had been restored to freedom in vain; his reason went, and he raved for some time after. Henry was in no generous mood when Curthose sent word to him for a parley; it was well past the time for talk.

Nevertheless they met, the brothers, at Cinteaux, between Falaise and Caen. They might have been strangers; Curthose was no longer the trusting creature he had been at Alton, even later on the hurried English visit when he had been shorn of his yearly allowance, supposedly to please the queen. Shortage of money now had caused him to fail, and he knew it: his men were unpaid and a few clung to him out of loyalty, their *droit seignor*. He was sullen and said little over two days, and nothing to the purpose. It was Whitsun, the season when knights are made by custom. No fire had come down from heaven, but he, Henry, had burned much of Normandy. In the end Curthose rode off, hunched in the saddle, a few still following.

Henry sat down in his tent and wrote to the archbishop to come to him at Laigle. The old man could still travel. He himself must make it clear who was master, both in church and duchy. A decisive battle would make the latter his; it could not be long now. As for Anselm, if he showed due humility he, the king, would restore him his see.

The king felt a sudden desire for men's company, and asked his crony Robert de Meulan to come, drink wine and talk of the Norman war. De Meulan – he was sparing in his use of the Leicester title, though he garnered every third penny of the county there – sipped wine, cautiously as he did everything. He had some time before arranged an advantageous marriage for one of his comparatively obscure birth; his countess had been Isabel de Vermandois, with the royal blood of France hot in her veins. Long since her husband irked her by his cautious ways, though she bore his sons and daughters, now grown.

The king turned his own wine-stoup in his fingers, with only half his mind on the talk. It seemed probable that the terrible Robert of Bellême would come to him in England in person, like a monarch, to talk of peace: and as though de Bellême had been a monarch indeed he dared not lay hands on him yet, but must listen. Patience, as usual, would achieve everything.

He waited in his great hall at Westminster, robed and crowned. He awaited thus the coming of Robert de Bellême, and watched, almost idly, the retreating procession of two hundred priests who had come to protest at their fines, imposed by him, for taking concubines. Henry had used the money for his Norman war. He played with the humour that he might provide young women to entice yet more priests; it was a notion that would have appealed likewise to Rufus, and there was nobody else with whom he could jest now about such things. For the first time, he missed his brother's loud irreverent voice, his laughter, his lack of cant. Nevertheless Rufus had had a religion of his own; the cult of chivalry. Time and again, in Normandy, he had treated released prisoners well, and had let them go free on their promises as knights. Prison could be a hard experience; Henry's old enemy William de Breteuil had died lately of a chill taken earlier, when he had been kept three months naked in a cellar open to the north wind, released only on the gift of his daughter to the gaoler, Goël of Bréval, with a dowry of three thousand pounds. Henry's old friend Robert FitzHamon was recovering somewhat in his wits from the head-wound at Dives, and his daughter had all of hers; Henry had offered Mabel FitzHamon his own son Robert as a husband, but the young woman had turned up her nose at first: Robert had no surname, she said. The king had accordingly given his son the name of Fitzroy, upon which Mabel remarked that he still possessed no lands. Henry then gave the couple the lands which should have been Mabel's by right in any case. The marriage seemed tranquil, and there were already children.

A clamour outside announced the advent of Robert de Bellême.

It was like waiting for the devil. The man strode into the hall with confidence, and nonchalantly enough for the king's mind to run over his immediate ancestry, which was most evil. His grandfather, who had cursed the Conqueror as he lay in his cradle, belonged to a religion which castrated its dinner-guests by unhallowed custom. De Bellême's mother Mabel Talvas, that latter man's daughter, had been famed as a poisoner and had bodily resembled a fat white slug; Henry recalled seeing her, horribly, in his childhood. Soon thereafter, old Mabel had taken a morning swim from her husband's castle of Bures, returning naked from the river to bed. Three brothers desirous of vengeance followed her inside, seized her by the hair of her head and cut the head off. They then escaped with it. Prayers for Mabel's soul were still being said in the convent of Troarn near Caen, but it was doubtful if they would have effect. As her son Robert advanced now, Henry felt the physical approach of evil, as if the man had imbibed it in his mother's womb. It was said that de Bellême sat laughing while his victims' eyes were gouged out, their hands and feet cut off; ransom was refused, for this Robert had enough money. He liked the spectacle of suffering in its own sake, the sound of screaming. He had imprisoned his wretched wife after the birth of their son. He was said to be unable to sleep, to trust no man; and yet he had designed glorious Gisors, also engines of war which had led to the capture of Jerusalem. He could have been an ally of great worth had he had honour, and a heart.

'I kneel to you as my overlord in England, but not in Normandy.' His robes made a rich rustling sound, with the chink of armour beneath. His face was inscrutable, the eyes betraying nothing. He rose to his feet after the homage. Henry said 'I could detain you, my friend, after Bridgnorth.' He had taken, at last, that castle, supposed impregnable; but it had cost many weeks, and the lives of men. De Bellême smiled.

'I think you will not. It would sound ill in Normandy for the king of the English to break his word regarding a man who returned to England in peace.'

'You are as peaceful as Flambard, doubtless.' The latter now was a respected bishop, sending prim complaints of the invasion of his forests by those who lived nearby.

'Well, Flambard escaped, did he not, from the Tower, by means of a rope hidden in a cask of wine? You see I forget nothing.'

'What do you want of me?' asked the king. De Bellême answered with a simplicity that did not belie him; he was given to bad deeds for lack of principle, and was greedy also.

'I would ask you, sire, to make me your chief vassal in Normandy. You yourself cannot hold two lands with the sea between. Once the king of France knows you to be more powerful than he, he will become your enemy; you yourself must have thought of it.'

A Lion of Justice shall arise who will make the lily quake as the aspen. 'And so?' said Henry equably.

'Let me call myself duke of Normandy, or count if you will. Your brother the duke reigns only in name. His servants steal his clothes and laugh at him. I would care for him, give him enough wine, and myself govern the duchy.'

He spread out the hands that had perpetrated unspeakable things; without gauntlets they seemed as other men's. 'I wish you well, but I will not treat with you,' said Henry. De Bellême seemed then as if smoke rose within him, and was silent for moments. Presently 'They say that if you wish well to any man, it means that you will destroy him,' he replied curtly, and went out.

Later Henry heard that he had already taken ship. He himself had made no attempt to detain the man; the time would come when he had de Bellême at his mercy, in Normandy.

2

DE BELLÊME HAD, thankfully, not waited to spend Christmas with them at court; the festival of Christ's birth was doubtless no part of him or he of it. Having heard that the man was, again, overseas, Henry himself rode north in the bitter weather to his old supporter Earl Simon's palace of Northampton. It was no less, being the appanage of Simon's young wife, whose father had been Waltheof of Northumbria, the last Saxon earl; betrayed mistakenly by his wife Judith and executed, though innocent of conspiracy, in the Conqueror's time. Simon, lame of a leg as he was, had greatly desired to marry the widow, who was niece to the king; but Judith's savage self-reproach had forbidden her to marry again, and instead she had given Simon her twelve-year-old daughter Maud with all of Maud's inheritance, which included this ancient Danish town and the great swathe of land which had once been the kingdom of Mercia.

Maud de St Liz had borne her old husband two sons despite his age and ugliness, and was herself a quiet, elegant and subdued creature. Simon meantime was not well, and already Henry looked out for a second husband for so great an heiress as Maud: he had already considered young David of Scotland, whom he could trust. David rode now in his train, saying little as usual, though what he did say was always agreeable. He had long been more of a Norman than a Scot, having been brought up at court since boyhood, when the Atheling had smuggled down the younger children of King Malcolm and Margaret at their deaths.

Henry thought briefly of his own queen, who had been one of those children; they were civil strangers to one another now, though Mald, as he had foreseen, was a help to him in signing writs and taking charge of matters in his absence. By now, he himself was increasingly unfaithful; he had lately at last tumbled old Robert de Meulan's young daughter Elizabeth, exasperated by her primness and long siege. Bess as a result was pregnant, like the Berkshire widow in her time; Ansfrida herself was by now long returned to the placid and unsuspecting acceptance of her neighbours. Henry smiled against the pervading February wind. Except for Mald, women went down before him like ninepins. However he had other things to think of at present; chiefly the election of two popes instead of one.

Maud de St Liz, Countess of Northampton and Huntingdon, fair of hair and complexion like her dead father Waltheof, greeted them with her two mannerly small sons, both progressing well under their tutors. Henry laid his hands on the boys' heads in fatherly fashion; after all his own Audelin was three years old now, and sturdy; unlike these boys he would be made into a fighter and strong ruler rather than a scholar; certainly there would be no question of his entering the church, as was already proposed for the younger of the boys, Waldef, his name modified from his grandfather's.

They entered the hall, feasted on what was set out hospitably ready, and sat later listening to a minstrel, near the blazing central fire which was welcome after so cold a journey, and rose high to the roof-hole. Henry was not greatly interested in music and legend, but sat civilly pretending to listen while privately perfecting his final plans regarding Archbishop Anselm.

The primate was, in his way, as persistent a source of trouble as de Bellême himself, and could summon forces as strong, if more beneficent. The matter of a second existing bunch of celestial keys must cause the good man concern. He had already written reproachfully from abroad to Henry for taking the money from priests regarding their concubines, and using it for his war. Presumably it should have gone to swell church funds. Anselm's people, and the bishops, had begged the archbishop to return to his Canterbury see, but he had replied that he could not do so without the king's permission. That, at least, was something accomplished; and Henry in turn has sent back word that he himself would cross to Normandy at Ascension-tide. There should, he thought, be a lively debate then; he himself preferred the papal candidate supported by the emperor, as that would outweigh the pretensions of France. Anselm undoubtedly would, for his own reasons, support the rival.

The minstrel finished his half-heard lay on a long, sad note; and Robert Curthose, duke of Normandy, walked alone into the hall.

His appearance was not only unexpected and unwelcome, but wild; his gait reeled, and his clothes had the appearance of having been flung on and to have belonged before that to someone else; the hem of his tunic lacked stitches and hung unevenly in places, and his linen was dirty. He was hardly the figure of a nobleman, let alone a duke and the brother of a king. His face had grown haggard, with the child's eyes staring out from it reproachfully. Henry rose to his feet.

'What are you doing here? Who bade you come?' It had been said before; no doubt de Bellême's safe return had encouraged his overlord to risk the voyage in person, even at this season. Curthose's hands clutched at his kingly brother's sleeve. David of Scotland had risen courteously also, but had already conveyed his hostess out of the hall. This, he knew, was men's business. Maud went obediently, her veil hanging in seemly folds about her slender figure. Both king and prince noted her with favour; it would surely not be long before her old husband died, and she was a very great heiress.

Henry sent word again to the archbishop that he would cross seas soon, with the news about two existing popes which Anselm would know already; but the point might as well be laboured. The king was grateful, as always, to his own father for having had him taught to write; it saved much labour both in the dictating and deciphering of the clear script few could yet fashion, even though Charlemagne, who had first had it introduced, was dead three hundred years, himself unable to write a word.

The king left Northampton, wishing the earl and his young countess well. He would have made ready to set sail, but affairs in England delayed him for some time after hearing that the archbishop was ill. Perhaps, he thought, the old man would die, in which case he himself would appoint a less stiff-necked successor. However, miraculously as was thought by many, the holy man recovered once more before the king set sail. Henry had meantime written part of the truth to Anselm, if not all of it; that his brother the duke had been to visit him, and had returned satisfied.

Anselm had found peace at Bec, his own former monastery where he had been fifteen years abbot, and before that prior under the saintly Lanfranc, who like himself had been called away in time to England to become primate under the Conqueror. Lanfranc, however, had had less trouble with that outwardly conforming king than Anselm had had with both his sons. The peace of Bec was disturbed when Henry's messenger came now in the person of the bishop-elect Warelwast, the same who had taken news of the Audelin's birth to Rome.

'The king desires that you return to England.' His voice was smug.

The king had formerly desired that Anselm did not return, or not till he had done certain homage of a kind he considered uncalled-for. However the archbishop had his own gear packed unwillingly, and set forth on the journey; he broke it at Jumièges, not feeling at all well.

He desired no welcome, and went alone into the great abbey with its springing arches, kneeling beneath them to pray, trying to forget the discomfort that had come upon him during the journey: it increased as he knelt. Within his head the blood pounded; he placed the white-haired head forward on his fine scholar's hands, and thought of the king despite himself while he tried instead to think of God, and of the nature of belief. It should come before knowledge; without it, all knowledge was vain.

Anselm knew, however, that Henry was a bad man but an able ruler, whereas Curthose was a bad ruler with an honest heart. For the country's sake there was no doubt who should rule Normandy in the end, though to have two lands separated by sea meant much travelling. It would end, no doubt, with the queen, whom Anselm loved greatly, becoming regent in England. He did not think that marriage had been happy, except at the first: but it had been necessary for the sake of the English people. They loved their Good Queen, but feared her husband.

No doubt it was God's will that the country should be ruled by Normans; they had begun near here, at Jumièges, where the son of old Rollo the pirate, first Patrician of Normandy, had greatly desired to become a monk, but had been refused admission because of his unchaste mode of living. After his murder, a chest in which he had said he kept his greatest treasure had been opened and found to contain a monk's habit of Jumièges. It had disappointed the murderers, who included his wife. There was much sin in the world, then and now.

The noise in Anselm's head had increased to a loud buzzing. Suddenly he fell forward, and those who had been secretly watching, to let the archbishop think he prayed alone, came in and lifted the old man's body and carried it into the monastery. Prayers were said and mass chanted; it was thought by everyone that the archbishop would die.

He lay ill for a month, then begged to be allowed to return to Bec. At that rate, the king had to go to him there. They met; discussed the matter of popes, of investiture, of lay against clergy, of Anselm's timely saving of the recorded English saints. 'The people are grateful to you for that,' said the king benignly. 'King Cnut himself stole the body of Archbishop Alphège from London out through the window of St Paul's, and had it conveyed by water to Canterbury with great pomp. England would not lightly have lost its saint.'

Anselm, who would be a saint himself one day, listened, tired to the bone. He could not argue any more; he agreed to return to Canterbury, and despite a rumour that he was already dead, passed over the sea on the day that followed the feast of the Assumption. He was greeted with joy at Dover. The king himself rode inland in Normandy, to make war on his brother the duke as he had long planned.

He had already begun to build a rival fort opposite the castle of Tenchebrai, held by Curthose's chief supporter after Robert de Bellême. This man's name was William of Mortain, a remote kinsman, and Henry marked him down for destruction. For one thing, de Mortain held a strong place. It was encircled by the Norman hills on one side and on the other, the hills of Maine. Henry expected reinforcements from there and from Brittany. He was aware of a certain excitement, alien to his precise cool nature; the expectation a hunter feels when he has sighted a stag. This stag should be brought down. By the end, when all this was over, he himself would leave two peaceful and powerful realms, in good order, to his son. The saying about the safely carried sack of gold was already being spread in England, also that he, the Lion of Justice, had arisen and would as prophesied make the lily quake. That necessity might not be obvious to the English, but they would learn. When he himself was in undisputed possession of England and Normandy – the situation was as clear in Henry's mind as a map – he would control as much land as the king of France himself, and with more seaports than the latter. That had not been his doing, but his old forebear Rollo's. Long ago, King Charles the Simple had thought to rid himself of the importunities of invading sea-pirates from the north by ceding them certain of his coastal lands for peace. As a result, all thriving seaports belonged to Normandy. Henry smiled to himself, watching the hills for action and remembering his dying father's word. 'Wait, and all will be yours.'

All should be his now, after this battle and despite William of Mortain.

Henry felt the sudden onset of violent rage of the kind his father had now and again exhibited. The subtle knight, William of Mortain, had tricked him. Not only had the Norman conveyed green forage into the besieged castle, enabling it to hold out for long enough in all probability, but had himself slipped in unnoticed, passing through the army the king had brought. The thought that he himself looked foolish as a result infuriated Henry. His voice roared out in anger; the main body must advance; the two armies must meet in battle without further delay, before winter.

He saw, on the peak of the hill, rival reinforcements come; Curthose himself rode at their head, his short legs making him easily recognised. Robert of Bellême stayed meantime near him, a sinister presence in black armour. The rebel abbot's son from Dives – the abbot had meantime fled to France, to become a tax-collector – was with them. Curthose spurred his horse down the slope; despite the fact that he was ageing now, no man could yet unseat him, and he knew it, regaining confidence now he was again in his own land, in the saddle.

'Raise the siege and depart peacefully, my brother, or else accept battle.'

The monks from the nearby monastery had come out, in a long trail of sad wailing. They begged the armies to depart without shedding blood. Henry heard himself speak above their beseeching, his voice trumpet-loud.

'Surrender all your strongholds, including Falaise; hand over half the duchy and the money made from fines and appeals to law. In return I will pay you the yearly revenue of the lands under my government.' He might, he had thought, otherwise be cornered; William of Mortain had tricks up his sleeve; they might well never win alive out of the embrace of the low hills.

Curthose said he would consider. Then some time later his envoys came. The offer was refused; he had taken counsel. 'Then it is battle,' the king said, and made ready. It was evident de Bellême ruled all.

He himself had, after all, been in tight corners before. The thing was to keep a cool head, to plan, even now, for the future, while the spears shone bright and couched for action in the autumn sun. He released, as a bribe, Earl Warren's brother Reginald, whom he had captured after the abbot's plot lately at Dives. 'Tell them I will rebuild their abbey,' he said. Then he turned to his men, and heard himself address them.

He had no memory afterwards of what he had said, except that he had memories of reading, long ago, Attila's speech to his

Hunnish invaders that they must conquer or die. Death had meant little to those alien invaders, who spent their lives as part of the horses they rode. He himself would dismount to fight; Robert's army on the contrary contained much horseflesh, its trappings gleaming among the assembled spears. The Saxons had a belief that no true fighter fought except on foot; well, he would take their advice, even though they had lost at Hastings for that very reason. The king came down out of the saddle, and ordered them to lead away his horse. Then he went about among the men, dividing the army evenly into three. Trusty Robert of Meulan commanded the first division, and the king shrewdly relied on Earl Warren himself for the second; that man should after all be grateful for the recent freeing of his brother. 'Fight as best you may,' he heard the earl shout. The men of Brittany and Maine, who had come, Henry placed in reserve; the scowling wild looks of the Bretons were alarming even while they stood inactive. He himself ordered the foot-soldiers; it should not be said that the king sheltered himself in war.

William of Mortain had sallied out of the castle; he was in command of the duke's first division. The second was in charge of de Bellême. In defeat, there would be no mercy.

The charge began, headed by William of Mortain and his men. There was soon confusion among the ranks of the cavalry, hindered as they were by their heavy accoutrements. Hélias of Maine, the famous leader, thundered from the king's side in to kill, his sword flailing about him. At sight of it, Robert de Bellême himself turned and fled. The forces of evil vanished after him as if in a black cloud, so many departing flies. Henry, fighting to right and left, smelling sweat and hearing clangour for the first time in long, was suddenly accosted by a priest, his chaplain Waldric.

'It is a victory,' panted the chaplain. He bore with him a prisoner, short-legged, dismounted and with his vizor still down. The duke removed his helmet, as their father had done at Hastings. 'I am your captive,' said Robert of Normandy. 'Do with me as you will.'

Henry ordered Curthose to be led away. Soon after, the old Atheling gave himself up. It was evident that he would not fight on without his friend, as Curthose had become. Henry received him courteously, remembering that after all he owed him his queen. A handsome young man, the king's own nephew, his sister Adela's son Stephen of Blois, brought in yet another captive, made by the Bretons; William of Mortain himself. With him, Henry would deal less kindly and knew it. He heard the chaplain speak.

'This victory has been won by your father's son on the fortieth year, to the day, after his landing at Pevensey,' he said. It was a sign, no doubt, of God's pleasure, as that first safe landing had been. Henry received word at once from his captive brother; he would yield possession of the fortress of Falaise, where his son was kept. It was possible that otherwise, Robert of Bellême would wheel about and seize it; and to have William Clito, the heir to Normandy, in de Bellême's hands was a fearful thought; better to lose the last strong place in the duchy.

Henry rode to Falaise, with the captive Curthose close by; and saw, for the first time, the dangerous boy the dead duchess had borne her lord. The six-year-old Clito was beautiful as the archangel on whose high rock he had been conceived, tall for his age and straight, with the sun shining on his thick long curls. Henry greeted the child, and his guardian, Hélias of Arques; and unlike himself as a rule was so greatly moved that he did not think, till later, how unsafe it was to have a son of Robert Curthose left in any hands but his own.

Curthose's final humiliation was at Rouen, when before an assembly of his former subjects he released them from their vows. Tears were pouring down his face. He had always, Henry thought, been prone to emotion. He himself was acclaimed by all present as king of England and duke of Normandy. He remembered the dying Conqueror's words; 'Wait, and you will win all.' It had happened, and with a final battle which had lasted less than an hour. He put Curthose in charge of his own son Robert, and saw him led away. William of Mortain, he who had conveyed the green forage, Henry ordered to be blinded. Not only might such an action have meant a long siege, but the knight had fought valiantly and had almost won a victory for the other side. That possibility must not be repeated.

Later, before the mass of thanksgiving held next day, Henry drank with his supporters; Earl Warren and Surrey who had fought against his own brother's men, Hélias of Maine who had saved the day; and that other, who had helped Waldric take captive the old Atheling Edgar, fighting unrecognised by all as he had been. The heir to all the ages could be given some manor or other in England, there to rot in solitude and forget his royal birth. Like the Conqueror before him, Henry found same the heir of all the ages too harmless to kill. The young knight who had aided the Atheling's capture, raising his vizor to reveal the handsomest face in the world, was after all one's youngest sister Adela's son. Adela was now in a Cluniac convent. Henry was taken with the boy Stephen and with his courage, and invited him to court; it was time he met his cousins. The certainty came to Henry that he must also obtain custody of the Clito, perhaps offer Curthose's son certain counties in England. Here, however, he met his match; the boy's guardians refused to give him up and took him secretly away by night, in the end to France.

Curthose himself was safely guarded, on his way to prison under the care meantime of the bishop of Salisbury. 'See that he has every luxury,' Henry had ordered, remembering Mont St Michel and the merciful gift of wine as well as water. He watched the short legs grip the saddle for the last time as his brother rode under strong escort to the port: and himself turned to issue edicts that all things in Normandy should again be as they had been in his father's time.

He knelt after mass in Rouen cathedral, less aware of the presence of God than of his buried ancestors not far off. Now, like them, he was duke of Normandy. There lay old pirate Rollo, the first Patrician, less destroyer than lawgiver, who had hung his famous gold armlet at last on a tree; he, Henry, would emulate him to the extent that a man in any of his dominions should be said to be able to carry a bag of gold from one end to the other without fear of attack. He would rule; better than William Longsword, Rollo's son, whose tomb was also nearby and who had craved in his time no more than to become a monk of Jumièges. They would not have him there because he had fathered a son on a Breton girl in his wars, and the son became Richard the Fearless, first duke of Normandy, who had married beautiful Gunnor of the many sisters, and had kept a stone coffin filled with corn for the poor at Fécamp, and now lay in it there, within sound of the sea. The sea was in their blood, his Norman race, its sound never stilled; he himself would cross from England time and again, and voyage back. He wondered how his son and Mald fared in England, and if Archbishop Anselm had yet received his letter about the decisive victory at Tenchebrai; he himself had made out the number of slain somewhat greater than they had been; there must be no doubt left in anyone's mind that Robert Curthose no longer counted even as a commander of men.

Henry crossed himself from habit, and rose from his knees, going out into the town's streets and the sunlight. The people did not yet cheer him; they had loved their duke, their *droit seignor*, inept and usually drunk as he was; and had heard, with sadness, that he had been taken away.

3

THE EPISODE OF Anselm's letter about the suggested de Warenne marriage to his daughter, and the encounter with young Stephen of Blois, caused the king to remember his own sisters, deliberately including what he recalled of Gundreda de Warenne. It was not much, although she had no doubt been present at Selby when his mother Queen Matilda had given birth to him there during the time she spent with the Conqueror in England. Gundreda was already by then the wife of the first William de Warenne, this present earl's father; and had died at Castle Acre in Yorkshire, in childbirth of a fifth baby who had died with her. Their double funeral had wound down the long way to Lewes, where Gundreda was buried at last in the Cluniac priory she and her husband had founded. After her death the old earl had married again, but had not lived long after supporting Rufus in Bishop Odo's rebellion, thereby gaining his Warren and Surrey title. Gundreda, therefore, had never been a countess. Henry tried again to forget her; he himself, by the time of her death, had been still in the monastic schools where his father had placed him in Normandy, learning his clerkly hand if little else.

Another sister, Constance, had died in childbirth in Brittany; she had been the wife of Alan Fergeant, who on widowerhood had become an early suitor of Mald, then still a young girl in Scotland;

and had witnessed the tearing of the nun's veil from her head by her father. Queen Matilda, their mother, had earlier prayed in vain for the life of Constance at Ouches, the fashionable convent where his own eldest remaining sister, Cecilia, was a nun. Nuns lived for long, being removed from the cares of the world. Adela, the youngest, having caused the death of her husband by sending him back to the Holy Land a second time after he had returned homesick, had brought up her sons and had then entered her convent, when they were grown. Of the rest, Alais, who had been promised to Harold Godwinson, had died on the way to unwilling marriage in Spain.

Now there were none of them left, accordingly; Richard, Rufus, both were gone; nobody remained for Henry to contend with except Curthose. At home, however, there still remained the recalcitrant archbishop, not yet dead.

The queen's brother Edgar, who had ruled in Lothian since their parents' deaths after overcoming an usurper with the help of his brothers, died in the January after Tenchebrai. Mald heard a mass for him with the feeling that it was being sung for a stranger. Edgar had been pious, and had remained unmarried all his life, ruling well enough; now, Alexander, who had helped him in the difficult north parts, would be king over north and south. She knew Alexander somewhat better; he rode often down, and had been on the great pilgrimage; also, two years back, he had ridden up the long new aisle of Durham on his magnificent Arab horse with its silver trappings, and had given it and them, also a suit of Turkish armour taken in the east, to the shrine of St Cuthbert. He had marvellous tales to relate of the saint's translation to the new shrine, the coffin being opened after five hundred years, part of them spent in a hot climate. 'He was incorrupt,' the queen recalled her brother saying. 'I would not have believed it had it been told me. The fine linen shroud the holy woman Verca wove adhered to his face, but the features could be seen through it; he had an upturned nose and a cleft chin. The abbot of Séez sat him up and pulled his ears and his feet, to the great horror of the monks; but there remained the proof of sanctity, and I am honoured to have witnessed it.' They had put the saint in his new shrine, and had forbidden women to approach it, which seemed odd when one remembered that St Cuthbert had made many friends of women in his day, including Verca herself. There was no doubt that the Roman rule, which their mother Queen Margaret had fostered in Scotland, had altered many habits since the days of the open-minded Columbans. However it was not her own place to question, or to do more in any way than obey.

The king immediately thought of a bride for Alexander, who alone among Margaret Atheling's sons had forsaken any vow of chastity and had already fathered a bastard son in the north he called Malcolm after his father. Henry had a daughter Sybilla, child of his mistress Sybil Corbet. The young woman was inclined to plumpness and wore her clothes badly, but perhaps the prospect of being queen of Scots, and of wearing King Alexander's matchless rope of pearls, got in the East as far as anyone knew, might induce her to take rather more interest in her appearance. Henry put it to the young king of Scots, who had reason to be grateful to him for hospitality. Alexander manifested no great excitement at sight of Sybilla, but agreed to the marriage.

'It is one more tie between our lands,' the king said to Mald when he next saw her; they were increasingly apart nowadays. 'You will have small trouble from the Scots while I am abroad, now my daughter is queen.'

She smiled, and accepted it. In his absences she would govern quietly, and seldom had to call in the powerful bishop of Salisbury, as arranged by Henry, for advice or aid.

Queen Sybilla bore her husband no children, and her father, learning of it and that she had not in other ways improved except for chastity, tried to atone to King Alexander for his barren and ungainly queen. The answer was personal success in war. The mountains beyond Abernethy had defeated his own father, in the Conqueror's day; opportunity should therefore be given to Alexander to aid him, Henry, in conquering others; the intractable Welsh ones. Otherwise, he himself had already had the notion of installing placid Flemings, his mother's race, on the west coast of that stubborn land, down at Pembroke. A remembrance came which Henry swiftly downed, of Rufus, standing alone on the coast there and looking across to Ireland. He would build, he had boasted, a bridge made of boats from one land to the other; but it had not happened. Henry smiled to himself, and went as usual to see his son and heir. Of his many bastards, only four were sons; the Audelin was doubly precious.

By the time the Audelin was five years old, a chance came to placate Archbishop Anselm by asking him to give the prince his blessing. Henry himself was staying at a royal manor near Portsmouth, waiting for a favourable wind to cross the Channel; he was more cautious in such ways than Rufus, who had been used to leap on the first available vessel saying no king had ever yet drowned. However the old prelate was too ill to come to them over the narrow arm of sea that separated them, though he was lodged not far off as the crow flew. It occurred to the king that an occasion might be made of it; he sent for his son, took pleasure in surveying the little boy's sturdy strength, and put him in charge of two churchmen who would at least point the moral that he, Henry, was anxious to mend matters regarding investiture and the disputed power of Rome. Rome had long ago kept Anselm himself waiting interminably for a hearing on that first matter, Rufus having, by a trick, been made openly to declare himself a supporter of Pope Calixtus, now dead; and the pope then had not dared risk losing the support of so powerful a ruler as England's king, godless or not. Now, here was a subsequent and more godly king, himself; had he had chosen Warelwast, still bishop-elect of Exeter, the same who had travelled to Rome to announce the Audelin's birth. The other was Giffard of Winchester, whose brother's widow might well in her time have poisoned poor young Duchess Sybil at Rouen. The king watched the two vested and mitred figures escort the child's small one into a waiting boat. It was, he thought, a presage of what must come; he must soon decide the fate of the church in England, suffering as it did from constant delay in decisions from so remote a place as the Eternal City, which he had fortunately not alerted with regard to the recent matter of de Warenne's marriage. The matter of investiture with ring and staff Henry had personally conceded, but there were still others; yet one could not unduly distress so holy and old a man as Anselm, or even openly wish him dead soon. The dispute, however, had already been echoed in Germany with the late emperor's wars, his famous snowbound penance, then a further war after that when Henry IV changed his mind. His son now was one's ally. The latter's future bride, the little princess Matilda, stood by now, watching her brother depart with the bishops in the boat.

Matilda – nobody any longer called her Aaliz – in fact nursed a faint grudge; she would have liked to go for the archbishop's blessing with her brother William and the bishops. At seven years old, she could just remember a time when she alone had been important. Now William was the Audelin, heir to England and, she was told, Normandy, though there was another William over there named Clito, which meant heir also. Matilda fingered her long hair, which they kept combed, washed and silken. Her father had told her she was to wear a crown. It could not be the crown of England. Matilda looked out on the calm sea, and thought how she had been told she must soon cross it to Germany, and learn a new tongue and new customs. Her name, as she already understood, would become Mathilde, the second time they had changed it.

The Audelin returned safely, with news of the frail archbishop who had blessed him, raising thin transparent fingers in the sign of the Trinity. The bishops conferred with the king, came to no conclusion, and went their ways.

Archbishop Anselm died at last in mid-May, shortly after having been entrusted with the official care of the king's son and daughter. This had been a mere civility on Henry's part to smooth over matters in general, including the continued putting off, by the stubborn Thurstan, suffragan archbishop of York, of any gesture whatever of submission to Canterbury. Thurstan's latest excuse was that he had written to the king in Normandy for permission. Although Henry was gratified at the implication that he had the final word, there was also to be considered the power lately given to Anselm from Rome to excommunicate both Thurstan and himself. To incur the ban of the church would adversely affect his own maturing plans for making the lily quake; an excommunicate was unlikely of support in war, and by now Henry intended to make it. Now, also, the late Anselm's revenues might with benefit be diverted meantime to the crown; he, the king, could plead the difficulty with York as a reason for not appointing a successor. He recalled that Rufus had been blamed for the same habit, and that he himself, at his coronation, had sworn to uphold the rights of the church and not farm out her revenues. However keeping them for himself was a different matter, in the same way as a deceased bishop's boots had lately been filled with the bishop's own gold and silver coin and transferred without delay to the royal treasury by Henry's officers. It was helpful to have as much money as possible after his English hogsheads of gold brought across to bribe the Normans. Moreover the war with France would be costly.

The lily itself was by now personified in the form of Louis the Fat, the prince who had visited Henry's court as a guest soon after the king's marriage. Henry recalled, with a certain justification, that he had refused a suggestion made then by the stout young man's stepmother, Bertrada, that he detain Louis prisoner in England. Bertrada had not only married a king who had a wife already, but herself had a living husband, the count of Anjou. It was a tribute to her beauty and persuasiveness that all three, king, count and herself had finally shared a bed for the night in complete amity after a banquet. Nevertheless those days were over, and Louis now was king of France. He was, in addition, the protector of the Clito, in itself an excuse for war. Curthose's son had been taken secretly from one castle to another, kept out of Henry's hands, by his tutor Tirel de Mainières and by Hélias de St Saens, which last had married a bastard daughter of Curthose and was loyal. Both men abandoned their possessions in Normandy, knowing well enough Henry would seize them in any case: and saw to it that France, Flanders and Anjou in turn hid the little Clito till he reached manhood. The heir's chief supporter, no doubt to anger Henry as much as from any desire to strengthen the child's cause, was none other than Robert de Bellême, that personage having recovered from his headlong flight at Tenchebrai. It would not be many years before a beautiful young knight, aged fourteen, rose from his knees before the king of France, his hair commendably shining in the sun.

Henry knew well enough meantime that Fat Louis, Fulk of Anjou and Baldwin of Flanders, the last famous for his great beard, were in unison to try to overthrow him not only in Normandy, but in England. Curthose's son, they had evidently decided, should sit on the Conqueror's throne instead of his traitor uncle.

Henry knew he would deal later with all of that. In the meantime, he was glad to have support from the German emperor, whose envoys came to kiss the hand of his little princess at Westminster. They came bowing stiffly, wearing great moustaches after the fashion of Eustace *aux grognons* de Boulogne at Hastings long ago. They knew little French and the converse had to be by way of chaplains, in Latin. However they were pleased with the princess's appearance and manners, left pledges, and departed leaving Matilda with the title of queen of the Romans. It was all that could be arranged at present, the emperor himself being occupied in troubles with his Staufen kin at home.

Archbishop-elect Thurstan then made everything easy by agreeing to bow to Canterbury when it should again have an appointed primate. Both he and Henry knew that the appointment would be delayed as long as was feasible. King, queen and queen of the Romans then went, with the court, to Nottingham for an important ceremony; and with them went, as always, Robert de Meulan, ready with advice: also Earl Warren and Surrey, still unwed.

The little queen of the Romans had been taught to write, and proudly appended her signature to the writ signed by her father the king, her mother the queen, and the great bishop of Salisbury as well as others, at Nottingham on the occasion of a new see being founded at Ely. It was the feast of the translation of St Etheldreda, who had herself been a princess, married twice; firstly to a fenland chieftain who respected her vow of chastity, and the second time to a little boy who happened to be king of Northumbria. On King Edwy's growing up he had sought a bride nearer his own age to take to bed, and Etheldreda had returned to her earlier contemplations and had died a saint, as could happen in those days without reference to Rome. Later her remains were found to be incorrupt and perfect, which disproved the story that she had died of a tumour of the throat caused by the worldly sin of wearing a necklace during her lifetime. Aaliz-Matilda fingered her own rich gear and reflected that the unseen German bridegroom she had lately married was hardly a little boy – she would have disliked that – but on the contrary a man older than her father. She looked round the assembly, seeing its gleaming vestments and mitres, especially that of the new bishop of Ely himself. King Edward the Confessor had gone to school at Ely as a boy, but it only had a bishop as from now, under her father, and not long ago a cardinal had come from Rome to consecrate the archbishop of York in St Paul's, by agreement with the king. Everything seemed to gleam, agreeably, with gold and to smell of incense; and she had been told that at her own German ceremony she must not be surprised if the bishop of Trier picked her up and carried her, as princes were not to be seen there to walk in public before the age of nine.

Behind her, among the king's company, Earl Warren and Surrey waited his turn to sign the charter. His thoughts were very different from a child's, and had never resembled such. He watched Mald's splendidly robed figure bend and sign, and thought how he had deliberately let the king make a fool of himself with Archbishop Anselm in order to obtain written recognition of his own mother Gundreda's standing; King Henry had caused it to be spread about that she had been a Fleming and no kin to the ruling family at all. Warren himself had already vowed that while the queen lived, he would marry no other woman. It was less out of desire for Mald's person nowadays – she was worn with penances, and her mouth had acquired a thin line with keeping the soft lips under control, as if she had to withhold her true feelings constantly – than for her lineage, as before. The Audelin lived, but was a child; and a child had before now been passed over for the vacant crown of England. The king himself was only a man, and accidents befell all men; and if the queen was left a widow who but he, Warren and Surrey, the king's assiduous counsellor and support since Tenchebrai, should step into the breach as her second husband? It was a dream, no doubt; but others had dreamed, notably the king himself. At the turn of the century Henry had been a landless prince in exile, fathering the galaxy of natural daughters some of whom were here today. Now he ruled England and Normandy, and France feared him.

Warren passed his tongue across his lips. He had a contempt for the men here who were about the king; they were new men, appointed by Henry from nowhere in particular. They were able, but lacked high birth. He himself, with Gilbert de Aquila whose father had fought alongside his own at Hastings, being the only Norman noble to be killed there, had no peers except, perhaps, a silent landowner from the north named de Brus; his family also came, in the first instance, from Normandy. Otherwise, there was only the inevitable Robert de Beaumont of Meulan, with his clerk's face and his discontented, high-born wife, who was again pregnant. So had her daughter Elizabeth recently been, by the king; the daughter she had borne him was still out at nurse. Young Waleran, the physically upright de Meulan twin, was making trouble in Normandy, having fortified two castles there on his own account. No doubt his mind was as twisted as his brother's body.

Warren surveyed Elizabeth's mother now: there was a handsome woman, mismated to so parsimonious and prudent a spouse. It was said Robert de Meulan only ate one meal a day. Countess Isabel was by blood after all a Vermandois, kin to the king of France. Failing the queen, and failing Isabel's existing, if uninspiring, husband, a match there might be highly desirable; but the other came first. There might perhaps be a providential accident to the king's royal person next time he travelled overseas.

The charter was signed, the bishops filed past the courtiers scattering blessings, and everyone went to dinner, which passed without incident except that someone at one of the lower tables made a coarse and familiar jest about the origin of the word Ely, which it was pretended nobody heard.

A distinguished company waited at Dover in the April cold to witness the departure for Wissant, where the emperor's envoys would await her, of the queen of the Romans, aged eight. Gleaming presents from her father and mother had already gone on board. The king and queen stood, furred and dignified, each with their separate thoughts; Mald was thinking that to send so young a child away to an unknown bridegroom overseas, much her senior and with a reputation for betraying his own father, was less than kind. However Henry had assured her that this was the best way of ensuring the success of the marriage while the bride's mind was pliable. Perhaps her own had not been, or not enough.

Henry himself was still inwardly ruffled over an episode which had taken place at Christmas. He had intended yet a further coronation on the grand scale, to emphasise both his final victory as duke of the Normans and the anniversary of the Norman dynasty as rulers of England. The Conqueror had been crowned on Christmas Day at Westminster in 1066; he, his son, would do the same now, as if Christ's birth were in some way aligned with the crowning of such kings as himself and his father. However the squabbles of two prelates had spoilt it. Old Archbishop Thomas of York, he whom Thurstan itched to supplant, being not yet dead though suffering greatly from the pain in his joints, had manfully been hoisted in the saddle and had ridden down all the way, prepared to conduct the ceremony; after all there was no existing archbishop of Canterbury. Henry had foreseen the occasion as breaking the precedent of crowning by a primate; after all Maurice of London had crowned himself in 1100, haste and the absence of Anselm then making it necessary. Unfortunately the present holder of the London title refused to give way in his own see, had created an embarrassing scene almost before the altar itself, and the coronation had had to give way to a simple mass. However Henry had been often crowned, would perhaps instead, for effect, make a point of leaving off his crown next Christmas, and even at Easter or Whitsun – at all of the great festivals. The very absence of the crown should remind everyone he was king, and he comforted himself that this second grand occasion, the sending off of his daughter with great ceremony to Germany, would occupy the watchers' minds in place of the late fiasco. He had taken, for her marriage in February, three shillings for every hide in England: they would remember that, at least.

The stately and handsome child who was to depart made ready to board the boat which had been earlier rowed in. The sea was calm for the time of year, the white cliffs clear behind her. She was happy to be the most important person in the assembly today, almost more so than the king her father; certainly more so than the Audelin or Richard, who as usual stood beside his half-brother. Robert of Caen, their father's son, watched Matilda kindly: despite the difference in their ages there had always been close affection between them. As for the queen, she was an obedient shadow, reft for today from her good works and her signing of charters and founding of hospitals. Once her eyes dwelt on her daughter, full of a kind of regret; they might not meet again, and she had not given the child enough love. As regarded the two boys, they showed no emotion; a girl was going away; girls didn't matter, at least till later on. They hadn't in any case known Aaliz-Matilda very well; her education had taken place separately.

The escort closed round the little shining figure with the wind stirring its long, well-tended hair, and the queen of the Romans was respectfully conveyed on board the anchored boat. The oars struck the water, farewells were said, and the child set out on a journey longer and more tortuous by far than the crossing to Wissant was to prove. However that no one on this April day could possibly foresee.

In August the king took Mald with him to Normandy. He had heard of growing ill-feeling on the French frontier, and the young count of Anjou, whose father had been friendly, had since the latter's death suborned the men of Maine who had aided Henry at Tenchebrai. Altogether the presence of a pious and high-born queen might persuade certain malcontents to reconsider, even to behave as chivalrously as Curthose had done at the time of Aaliz-Matilda's birth.

The sea glimmered blue and calm; the crossing was smooth, their welcome at the port undoubted. Mald in the days that followed accompanied her husband decorously on all public occasions, causing murmurs of approval among the Rouennais. She herself was not happy. For one thing Robert de Meulan was forever in attendance, and that meant his daughter Elizabeth, who had left her child by the king at home. The queen treated the young woman civilly, for Mald was never uncivil; but she failed in any case to feel at home in Normandy, where their high and arrogant ways were alien to warm remembered England and its friendly people. The queen returned as soon as she could, giving the excuse that she had promised to extend a fair of eight days relating to the abbey of Malmesbury. It was St Aldhelm's fair, an old Saxon devotion. The king saw her off with ceremony and some relief, and himself spent Christmas with Bess in Normandy.

He had several matters on hand other than Elizabeth de Meulan. For one thing, the count of Flanders with whom he had completed a friendly treaty was dead like old Angevin Fulk, and a successor might well support the Clito. That angelic personage also appeared to be a protégé of Fulk the Young, as he was known, of Anjou; he himself was the son of wicked and beautiful Queen Bertrada by her first marriage to his father, Fulk of the Wry Mouth, he who had ended amicably in bed with her and her subsequent spouse the late King Philip of France. Changes had been rung in all places; Henry had to keep his mind more than usually supple to deal with them. He learned, for instance, that Fulk of Anjou proposed to marry his daughter to the Clito in due course; that would not do, the counties of Anjou and Maine could tip the balance between Normandy and France, and Fulk the Young had already married the available heiress of Maine.

Henry employed his usual weapon, gold. It so happened that the present pope was his own remote cousin through the inescapable Duchess Gunnor. The king set matters in train to stop the Clito's betrothal, persuading the pontiff to plead consanguinity; that could always be proved somehow, if one looked far enough back. Henry recalled the instance of Earl Warren, which had taught him a lesson; now, he would seize the weapon that had been used against himself. Many in Normandy remembered the Clito; for the boy to have possible rights to Anjou and Maine as well would be disastrous, though Fulk's wife had lately borne him a son named Geoffrey, said to be very handsome.

The game of chess continued. At home, Mald wrote that old Earl Simon de St Liz of Northampton was dead. That left his widow free to marry her youngest brother David; there would be no objection from either party, and a new young earl in charge of the Midlands, who had cause to be grateful to himself, would be an asset to Henry on that particular front and possibly others.

He arranged that; and about then a second singular piece of good fortune overtook him. The king of France, Fat Louis, foolishly sent an envoy to Henry who was none other than Robert de Bellême in person. The king, without hesitation, seized the envoy and sent him to England under strong escort, to be warded for life in Wareham. Louis would doubtless not be pleased; but the capture of so strong a foe was worth anyone's displeasure. One could, in course, at a predictable time meet and charm Louis. It had been done with others. The possibilities of action on this side of the Channel were limitless, and with England quiet under Mald, the bishop of Salisbury and by now Earl David, he himself might proceed with his growing territorial ambitions almost unhindered.

In the year after their marriage the former Maud de St Liz bore her new husband, Earl David, with whom she was happy, a fine little son. They named him Malcolm after the old king of Scots. While Alexander aided King Henry in Wales, the couple rode north to hearten the Scots by the sight of a future heir. Alexander's queen was still childless, and not greatly liked.

They rested at Rescobie, intending to ride further north; and there an unspeakable thing occurred. Old Donald Bán, the former usurper, who had been blinded, was kept there, and somehow gained access to the little boy and strangled him. The news came to Mald in London and to Henry at Rouen. Earl David's gentle wife was already pregnant again at the time of the child's death, and the news did not make her miscarry; but she bore a daughter. It was Maud's fourth child by two marriages, and she was not young. The only hope was through prayer; and it took her through yet another daughter's birth to, at last, the fine heir they named Henry after the king of England, and who would become known in time as Henry, Earl of Huntingdon.

Before then, King Henry himself had cozened the king of France to meet him to talk peace at Gisors, the great castle Robert de Bellême in his time had rendered impregnable. Louis brought with him Fulk of Anjou, by now Henry's secret ally. Neither man mentioned the reason; Fulk had been persuaded to betroth his other daughter, Matilda of Anjou, to the Audelin without making the matter known: the bride was still very young. How the argument was to be sustained that no consanguinity existed on this occasion was neither apparent nor yet thought of, except in the fertile brain of the king of England. Henry had, naturally, planned everything of the kind long since.

Elizabeth de Beaumont slid naked into the king's bed. She was obeying instructions from her father that Henry must at all costs be kept contented. Robert de Meulan never ceased from his attendance about the royal person, assiduous with advice, his increasingly yellowed face bent forever over the tall royal shoulder. His father, before that, had advised Queen Matilda when she was regent for her husband King William, in Normandy in the years following the Conquest. It was, accordingly, a family tradition to serve; although young Waleran looked as if he was about to depart from the lines long laid down.

Elizabeth felt the king's weight turn upon her, her own face in the dark already grown a trifle sour. If it wasn't for being his mistress, or one of them, she could have been married long ago. As it was, the king himself had arranged an excellent marriage already for their little daughter, with Gilbert de Clare. The prospect of the earldom of Pembroke was a tempting one, by now beyond Elizabeth's own touch. Her touch, instead, was evidently this stoutening man's flesh, forever avid and lecherous; she herself had perforce had to learn many whore's tricks over the years. She used some now, hearing Henry's thick grating laughter.

He grunted finally, and Elizabeth felt her loose mouth smile; it had once been prim, a young girl's with a tight virginity which had had to submit to painful royal deflowering. She didn't want to conceive by Henry again, and prior to coming to his bed always took a brew concocted by the advice of a certain wise woman. Its bitter flavour was still on Elizabeth's tongue. It was part of her hold over the king, such as it was, that she didn't cost him more money for the upbringing of yet more children. His others thronged the court, and marriages had to be arranged for them.

Their twined bodies, the man's and the woman's, had sunk deeper by their own weight into the softness of the provided furs. The drawn curtains shut in any sounds that came next time, and the next; he was demanding, the king. Elizabeth had ceased to think during all of it, Henry never. While satisfying himself physically to the fullest extent, he felt his mind work smoothly like oil. Carefully, while thumbing the Beaumont girl, he was planning the next move against King Louis and the Clito. The latter was almost beaten, and had written humbly of late to ask that he might take his father and go with Curthose to Jerusalem, never to trouble the king more this side the Alps. Henry had not yet replied and might not trouble to do so. He rolled off his mistress, sated, at last; and felt her leave him, huddling on her gown again beyond the curtains.

Pembroke itself had been in Henry's mind for other reasons than its earl. With Normandy under his control, and beginning again to resemble the form it had known in the days of his father, he remembered that he was part Flemish through his mother and that he had already established a colony of Flemings on the remotest part of the Welsh coast. In the first place they had been mercenaries, brutal as such men are and without hope for the future: but given the chance of daily living they had married on the allotted lands and settled down. The admixture of thrifty Flemings with fierce Welsh brides was successful; crafts began to flourish, the languages to merge as Saxon was already doing with Norman, and the region itself was already known as England-beyond-the-mountains. Moreover Henry had at last persuaded two bishops to stay, differently from the timid Hervey who had accordingly had to be removed from Bangor to Ely in the famous year of Aaliz-Matilda's marriage to the emperor.

The Welsh mountains still challenged the king, as they had his father; and by 1114 he had been able to persuade Alexander of Scots to march with him there, leaving the latter's brother David and his new bride to their tragic journey between Huntingdon and Scotland. There was peace in all his lands, except among these mountains, where chiefs ruled as they would. This had been the case since the first coming of the Saxons; the earlier race of Celts had fled westward, to Wales and Strathclyde, Brittany and Ireland. They were a distinct people, dark, poetic and moody, warlike when opposed. The legendary Arthur had been one of them; so had the early Conan Mériadech, king of the Bretons, who had killed the last Druids there including their priestesses, nine of whom had taken shelter on an island and had in the end been slain with fire, water and the sword, three to each fate.

Such images rose in Henry's mind as he rode, alone at the head of his men, as Alexander had meantime gone by a different way. They had sent three armies together against Gwynedd, and now he was crossing the Berwyn mountains in person. He expected hospitality from Rhys ap Tudor, reigning prince of Deheubarth, in order to make peace.

The prince greeted him, and gave him shelter and food. Rhys also had a daughter; and never in his life had Henry so greatly desired any woman at first sight.

Her name was Nest, and the intimacy of the word itself amused him. She had the power of a witch, the fascination of the lost sorceresses of Celtic myth; Branwen the high-born of sad fate, Morgan le Fay who had incestuously ruined her brother Arthur; the wicked princess Ahès who brought about the drowning of the city of Ys at the whim of the devil. He could not have described any feature in especial that made his member rise at very sight of Nest the princess, only that he must at all costs possess her, and at once. After dinner he demanded that she be sent him; his men-at-arms would quell any opposition by her father. Perhaps the notion they had here that a guest was sacred allowed, in any case, this favour as well.

She came, her light gown hushing in the draught of warm air that came up from the hall; her long hair was loose under a fillet. She was smiling with closed lips. He knew he was in her power, rather than she in his: and in his turn, as he had caused to happen to so many women in his time, felt his limbs grow weak with desire. Her eyes, the unfathomable eyes of the ancient half-vanished race, regarded him boldly. It was evident that she knew very well what was to happen; had known from his first coming, their first meeting.

'Who can disobey the king?' he heard her say softly in Welsh. The last sounds of the bard, who had sung to them at the high meal, sounded from the hall below, then died. By then, he had seized her, knowing he would have taken her, willing or not; and although he had not understood the words she said, he knew she was willing.

They copulated notably, the night through. Nest was not a virgin, nor had he expected to find her one. He mouthed her naked breasts and bit her underlip, enjoying her agreeable writhings. He found himself ejaculating into her, before the end, without let; he had early determined to leave a remembrance of himself within her. The hours passed in his repeated taking of her, the familiarising of himself with each separate and intimate part of her body. He had never given himself as totally to any woman, nor taken one as fully. He knew he was bewitched, that this was a second Delilah, and that if she were to demand his secret of him he would give it her; he could deny her nothing. Nor, as was not customary to him in his expected transports, could he think of anything but Nest's presence, the beguiling smell of her flesh against the pressure of his avid nostrils. He kissed many times the secret, light-downed place which gave her her name, fondling and entering; dawn came to find him still desirous, still coupling and kissing.

He sojourned in her father's stronghold for some time, feeling it after all a reward for all he had achieved, the chastising of France, the fall of Robert de Bellême, the defeat of the Clito, his own triumph everywhere. There followed, at last, the homage of the native princes of Gwynedd. He hardly heeded them, or the pious disapproval of the rejoined Alexander of Scots. Alexander had come upon Henry in the Welsh princess's bed at noon, and had seen in it an insult to his sister; that could not be helped. Nest's responses were fuller and more lasting than Henry had ever encountered in any woman, here or abroad. His own lust grew more open, more demanding, less quickly stilled. It could be said of him that he could not leave the Welsh princess alone. They could say what they chose, he decided. The nature of the woman who had borne Alexander's natural son in the north would be known to no one. He himself had continued determined to get Nest with child, and that its paternity should be known to all.

By the time he left, he knew that he had contrived it. The thought of her neat little belly's swelling over the months of his enforced absence was gratifying; for the present he rode south, Alexander north to meet the sad news of the little child Malcolm's gruesome death. As soon as it might be done, he, Henry, would send for Nest to come to court. Other matters intervened before he heard of his son's safe birth to her and that the child was to be named Henry. Almost by the same messenger, he heard that Nest was married.

The news infuriated him. Her chosen husband was the doughty Gerald of Windsor, a vassal Henry dared not offend. Earlier, before Pembroke was safely occupied under the Flemings, Gerald had defended the castle there. The king however ground his teeth at thought of their marital embracings, especially as Nest proved speedily once again with child. That also was born safely, but the king heard yet more in time to sour his expectant mind; the Welsh princess was thereafter carried off by her own cousin, Owen ap Cadogan, who took her about with him and kept her firmly on her back. Two years later, in Normandy, Owen was finally killed by a vengeful Gerald, and Nest was returned to Wales, perhaps the wiser for three strong men's incessant attentions. Her son Henry Fitzroy came to court, to be brought up there with the rest. More than ever the king could be spoken of as a second Solomon. He had returned, however drearily, to Elizabeth de Meulan, almost as though she were an accustomed wife.

By the end of September, Henry was on board ship at Portsmouth. He and the Audelin waited, in adverse weather, till the beginning of the month, then set sail. The king knew he would spend Christmas in Normandy; also, by the new year, would cause the barons to swear fealty to his son at Rouen.

He watched the pride of Normandy, sons of the men who had sailed with his father, kneel one after the other to his son. Pennants flared, bearing devices now that had not been thought of then; the scene was one of shining mail and coloured trappings, with swords sheathed for the time. Henry watched with pride his sturdy Audelin, accepting homage, bearing in his veins the blood of the old kings and the new. William III would found a fine race. The bride had been chosen; Fulk the Young of Anjou had been cozened afresh to promise his daughter, having taken the other away from the Clito on persuasion: that young man was a beggar, dependent on the bounty of others beyond the border, hardly remembered today: so the king told himself. Beside the Audelin stood Stephen of Blois, the likeable lad who was Adela's son; the cold light shone on his bright hair. Young Richard was still with his tutors; Mald mothered him at home, and he had not come with them on this occasion. As a rule the two boys were close.

Henry felt himself, on this day, increasingly a watcher, no longer a part of events. He had planned them and they had occurred. He had made himself king and duke in order that his son might be king and duke, and he had made his son, and his son would make a dynasty. He looked on all of it, like God, and saw that it was good. Never again would the flame of bodily passion burn in him as fiercely as it had done in Wales, and Henry Fitzroy was no more to him than his other children. Of them all, Robert of Caen, got in youth, was perhaps the most dear to him; but Robert after all was not the heir. The heir came down in procession now, with dignity and wearing a small gold circlet and long cloak. The king himself no longer felt it necessary to wear his crown on all occasions, except in war. One young noble bore up the Audelin's rich mantle, another carried his sword: beyond, the common people gaped and murmured. They must in fact accept his son, the king thought, as they had in principle accepted the Clito. They must forget the Clito's father Curthose, held safe in England in prison: their *droit seignor*. He himself should perhaps have ordered wine to flow, to loosen their mood; but in any case he had the whip hand, so it did not matter.

The queen of England stood by her new bridge at Bow, built in an arched fashion seen for the first time in England. The river Lea flowed in docile manner beneath today, unlike the time she had been caught in its high flood. Those who desired to travel north or south might do so now without trouble or danger. Bishops' blessings had sounded, scent from the incense spread itself through the waiting air, and the folk had left Stratford market, with its Cheshire cheeses and salt port and milk to drink straight from the cow, and leather and nails to be bought, to come for themselves and see the Good Queen, standing patiently as always to hear petitions and to do good where it might be done. She was known never to turn anyone away. She wore bright garb as always, her face worn with secret penances beneath the close caul and crown. Within herself she was tired and sad. Her sister Mary had died lately, far away in Boulogne. None of their mother's children seemed to live to be old. There was the young daughter, called Matilda after herself; and Matilda of Boulogne would be a rich heiress.

What did riches matter? Mald looked across at the thing she had accomplished; the bridge, and there had been roads also made by her, with calvaries in the Breton manner raised every few miles along them so that anyone might stop when they would, and pray. They blamed her, no doubt, for having these crosses gilded, saying the money could have been better spent; also that she had raised certain rents from those who could well afford it, to pay for the sick in St Giles-in-the-Fields and Christ Church hospitals; and, as always, bread, meat and wine, the best that could be bought, for the poor and hungry.

Henry after all spent more on his wars than she did on her charities; that, no doubt, was to be expected. However other things troubled her. The archbishop of Canterbury had been elected at last after five years, but Thurstan of York had asked permission to go to Rome, and the king had refused; and had sent rascals like Ranulf Flambard, reinstated long ago in Durham as well as Normandy, to go to Thurstan and persuade him to accept consecration at the hands of the primate. Thurstan had refused, and there had been an altercation of the kind witnessed long ago one

Christmas, when Henry had wanted to be crowned again at Westminster and had had to do without, as two bishops almost came to blows before the altar. That had been for reasons of less import than those emerging now.

Her mother would have been firmly on the side of Rome, she knew; Margaret Atheling had swept away the lingering cobwebs of the old forms of religion in Scotland, and had not been liked there for it; but here in England it was difficult not to form opinions favourable to St Augustine, who had come from Rome to Canterbury long ago. Had it not been for Rome then, England might well have remained pagan; yet in the north the faith had returned by way of Ireland and Iona. David her brother had told her there were Columban monks still in hiding in the forests despite the decree at Whitby which should have made them conform to the Roman rite four centuries ago: yet St Hild herself, at that time merely the great abbess in charge of proceedings, had voted otherwise then, being anxious to leave things as they were. Down here, it was different now; Henry, and his brother before him, tried to take to themselves, as kings, the power of decision regarding the church, and one could not condone it. She herself, unlike her mother, had no influence of that kind, and must say nothing; she could only pray.

How tired she was! She had a dragging pain which had troubled her for some time, and had accepted it silently as part of Christ's sufferings. If Henry came back to be with her at Christmas, as he had promised, she might perhaps tell him she was not well; that was not for her own sake, but in case he unwillingly left the land without governance if she should die when he was away. As it was, she had been his regent often. Robert of Caen, his son, had helped her greatly, and the bishop of Salisbury who held poor Curthose in durance. She had not dared aid her godfather, Henry's imprisoned brother; but, again, remembered and prayed for him always. In the end, God would make just reward. Soon, in any case, her son would be old enough to be left in charge himself. It was some time since she had seen William Audelin: his father undertook his education and always had.

Life, after all, was a making of bridges. She left the one at Bow, and turned to where her litter waited, having given away her last silver coin for the time. The pack-mules started, the litter swayed as the Good Queen lay, smiling and raising a thin hand here and there in blessing. They progressed between waiting crowds back to Westminster, and the white-painted chamber, and the ministrations of her women; still the same faithful three who had been with her since her marriage, and who would watch her die: Gunnhild, Christina, and Emma.

4

THE WARLIKE BISHOP Thurstan of York was causing more trouble in his way than Anselm had ever done in his, and at one point had stamped his foot and resigned his see. The pope however had restored it to him, and Henry, between popes and bishops – the pontiff who had been his own remote cousin was dead, having been placated at Gisors, and a new one had to be dealt with who proved slightly less amenable, in fact threatening to place England under interdict if Thurstan were not restored – was weary of the strife and not in fact greatly interested in the rival claims of Canterbury, London, York and Rome; what he intended was to secure power for the crown. Meantime, he left things as they were and, in Normandy, absently fondled Bess de Meulan now and again to relieve his physical needs. He had newly risen from her when a summons came for him of tidings from England. He went to the hall, leaving Elizabeth to pull down her rumpled skirts; she had noted glumly that, as a lover, the king was not what he had been; he had taken too many women, no doubt, for too long.

The messenger waited with a grave face. 'Sire, it is the worst news. The queen is dead. She was not ill for long.'

Henry stared out at the May sunshine. 'Have they buried her? Have masses been said?'

He was told that they had, and that the queen was buried at

Westminster. None of it seemed real. He found himself lying prone on the floor, a supplicant; also, it was a position in which none would disturb his supposed grief. He was aware of regret for having lain with a mistress while the news came from the coast, but no stronger feeling. At the same time, he knew that, with Mald, there had perished the last of those informed about the truth of the New Forest murder. Tirel de Poix, Robert FitzHamon, William de Breteuil, all were dead; and now Mald herself was so. No doubt she and Rufus had already met in the shades, wherever dead souls found themselves. She had been a good woman, when all was said, and had borne his son.

He rose at last, and went to tell the Audelin. 'Also, send word to my daughter in Germany.' The last news he had had from there however seemed to imply that Aaliz-Matilda and her husband the emperor were no longer in that land at all, but across the Alps in Italy. A messenger would find them, wherever they might be.

He turned away on his errand, head still bowed as if in grief. In fact he still felt none; it was a long time since he and Mald had meant anything to one another, if they ever had done. The marriage had been of importance, because of her descent. That survived in his children. There was little more to be said. He found himself, oddly, remembering almost the last thing he had heard about Mald; that she had caused the chains to be struck off a man imprisoned in England for concealing treasure trove.

In his own place of Bellencombre, the earl of Warren and Surrey also heard the news. He looked out for instants at the Varenne river from which his family took its name, a name by far more ancient than that of the dukes of Normandy. He had kept close about the king of late months, leaving no doubt as to his own continued allegiance; now, it was time to redeem his promise to himself that he would marry no other woman during the queen's lifetime.

He took horse and rode to Meulan, where the countess and her younger children were. Robert de Beaumont himself, the king's assiduous adviser, was not well; his yellow colour had deepened of late months, and he was absent now on the king's business. Warren went to the countess, who knew him well enough by now; took her by the wrist, and led her up to her husband's empty bed. There he lay with her, and his determined purpose intrigued even a mother of five; after dull Robert, the embraces of such a man were welcome. Countess Isabel made no demur when Warren took her away, out of reach, with her young daughters. He feasted her notably at Bellencombre, feeding her there like a fattened partridge, differently from the stringent diet she had endured from the beginning with her abstemious lord. At nights they made love. By the time Isabel was pregnant by Warren, her first spouse tactfully died.

The pair were married, and the king, professing shock and perhaps even feeling it, demanded the custody of the Beaumont children, though the elder boys were no longer incapable of decisions of their own. Henry took Robert the hunchback boy, and young Hugh, to court to be reared by him there. Waleran stayed for the time being with the man who was by now his stepfather; the marriage had taken place without delay, and Warren and Surrey was able to add the Vermandois fesse checky to his armorial device. It was almost as important a marriage as if he had wedded the queen. Soon he returned with his bride to Lewes, where his heir was born; and concerned himself for a time with the affairs of his townsfolk, their fairs and the support of the great Cluniac foundation started by his parents. Once he rode north to Castle Acre and stood among his own great earthworks there, surrounding the little stone house in which his mother Gundreda had died. It nestled like the inner whorls of a shell, nearby the small priory which was an extension of that built at Lewes. Warren prayed for her soul, and for that of his father, who when dying had dreamed that he was being carried off by devils. No doubt all men were the same, and came to the same end.

Meantime, Robert de Meulan was buried in the chapter-house at Préaux, where his sister was abbess. The king would have to continue without his advice, which had always been prudent, as expected.

Apart from cozening the pope at Gisors, Henry continued at once to make war on France and to seize opportunities regarding it, perhaps more rashly than if Robert de Meulan had been alive. The king built fortresses at Malassis and Gête, and seized Claire-sur-Epte, where his ancestor the old pirate Rollo had long ago made a treaty with Charles the Simple and had, so they said, tipped the king backwards off his throne by seizing Charles's foot when asked to kiss it in homage, saying he was damned if he would kiss any man's foot. Nevertheless at a pause in hostilities, Henry saw to it that the Audelin knelt in due homage as a vassal of France. King Louis' fat face brooded palely, but he could neither seize the duke of Normandy's son in turn nor refuse him. By then, despite the continued vacillations of Fulk the Young, it was certain that Anjou and Maine were on the side of Normandy against France. Nevertheless there were annoyances; Louis burned Laigle, where once an eagle's nest had been disturbed at the building of a castle by a supporter of the Conqueror, and since then the king had met with Anselm there. While still angry at the burning, he was informed that Rouen itself was being attacked by Hugh de Gournai, Edith de Warenne's son by her first marriage, and that a castle was being thrown up in defence on St Catherine's Mount. Henry made a forced march to his Norman capital, only to find that the report had been untrue. Still angry, he laid siege to de Gournai's lands and burned the town of Neubourg. Robert de Meulan would have advised discretion by then: but Robert was dead.

In all these enterprises the king was cheered by the presence of his nephew young Stephen of Blois, whom he came to like and trust increasingly.

He had made good marriages for his illegitimate daughters. Among them was that with the count of La Perche, who had married one of his Matildas. She was a friendly girl who was a favourite with her half-brother the Audelin, and was often at court. Different still was Juliana, whom long ago Henry had married to de Breteuil's bastard, Eustace. By now the couple had two daughters he had never seen and had no desire to see. He forgot the matter in the renewed affair of Bishop Thurstan of York, who dared to visit him in Rouen on the way to Rome. As the bishop lacked his, Henry's, permission to travel there, he detained him. No doubt trouble of some kind would follow.

It was in November that he led a renewed attack on Laigle, with the brothers of Blois, Stephen and his elder, Theobald, beside him. In an assault on the castle he was almost killed when fighting an action against King Louis. The latter had been defeated by Henry's order to his men to shoot at the horses rather than the knights who rode them. The horses fell dying, the knights were taken for ransom; and Louis, who had escaped, wandered stout and disconsolate in a forest, having lost his way. Before he found it, Henry himself was attacked by a fierce blow on the head from a knight of France who loathed him, and knew him by his crown, worn always in battle. The blow would have killed the king but for his helm, which saved him. The assailant, de Crépi, was with difficulty prevented from being torn in pieces for sacrilege. The battle had been a small one, smaller even than Tenchebrai. By then, Henry's sons fought by his side, one of them the young Audelin. On the other side was the Clito, supporting France. Henry sent back the king of France's horse unhurt, the Audelin did likewise with his cousin the Clito's charger; and for the only time, the two had sight of one another, standing in clear light on the field. No words were exchanged; the survivors went their ways after the combined brief nod to chivalry, and never met again.

The king and his nephew Warren and Surrey had this in common; they could hold long grudges, and bide their time. Henry had never forgotten how William of Breteuil had ridden after him and tried to prevent his initial seizure of the treasury at Winchester, proclaiming as his own liege lord Robert of Normandy and almost losing Henry the crown. Before that, de Breteuil and his family – they were, like most others of high blood from the duchy, descended from a sister of Duchess Gunnor – had prided themselves on being as greatly responsible for the conquest of England as the Conqueror himself. Their father was still remembered as Proud Spirit, having goaded the cautious Norman baronage into following its duke in what seemed to many like a mad adventure, an enterprise beyond seas whose success was in strong doubt. Perhaps it was a judgement on de Breteuil the younger that he left no legitimate heir. Henry had married the man's bastard, Eustace, to his own least favourite natural daughter Juliana; the two would, he thought, make a pair. They had two young daughters only, by now almost of an age to marry; he had not even yet set eyes on the girls, who had remained in Normandy.

It so happened that he had given in charge the strong tower of Ivry to one de Harenc, a knight he favoured. De Breteuil's daughters were in residence there and their father demanded it back.

'Give me your son as hostage, to ensure peace,' the king had said to de Harenc. The boy had been handed to de Breteuil accordingly, and Henry rode off to pursue his wars. Only later did he learn that de Breteuil, and his friend de Montfort, kin to Queen Bertrada, still clamoured for possession of Ivry. When it was refused they had torn the de Harenc boy's eyes out of his head and sent them to his father on a dish.

Henry was greatly enraged. The episode touched on his personal honour. He had handed over the boy in good faith. He felt the rage boil blackly in his blood; they should not treat him with impunity because that honour was involved. His two granddaughters were still in Ivry. The king gave de Harenc permission to take such revenge as he could devise. The two girls were blinded by de Harenc and had their noses slit. The king shrugged when he heard. Those two would be unfit now for life in anything but a convent; it ended the proud line.

The outraged father did not fail to strike back. De Breteuil fortified four castles against Henry and sent a contingent of knights to his wife to defend Breteuil itself. He had however reckoned without the townsmen, who were not anxious to make an enemy of the powerful king who was by now also duke of Normandy. They opened the gates, leaving Juliana under siege in her husband's castle. Henry lodged himself in the town, and waited. Shortly he received a message from his estranged daughter, asking that she be permitted to receive him.

He went, in full armour and remembering the ambush at Dives. He had not seen Juliana for some years, had taken little note then, and hardly knew her now. She had coarsened, in the way older women will, and her face was still swollen with tears at the ugly fate of her children. She did not kneel to her father; instead, her red-rimmed eyes flashed sudden fire, and she threw a javelin with all her strength, having concealed it behind her back. 'You bloody devil,' she screamed. The strength, a woman's, had however not been enough. Henry caught the javelin expertly as it whistled through the space dividing them. His hands were still precise. He laughed.

'I will not turn it on you,' he said to the cowering woman. 'I will let others punish you in their own way; never say your father is unmerciful.'

'Kill me, for God's pity. How can I live now? You have ruined my children, my pretty children.' She had begun to wail, her mouth a black cave, lacking teeth. Suddenly she would have gone for him with her nails; he stepped aside, slapping her lightly on the cheek. He used the javelin's butt to defend himself till he had won back beyond the gates; it was hardly necessary, the folk were afraid of him, this tall grim king in mail, wearing his crown and closed vizor.

'Destroy the drawbridge,' Henry said. 'Let all of them in.'

He watched the demolition of the drawbridge, the taking of Juliana's servitors, with coolness. Anyone who chose might enter now; might rape the lady of the castle, steal her clothes and her rings; mercenaries had small mercy. 'If she wants to escape it will have to be by sliding down the outer walls,' he told them calmly.

The notion appealed to them. They had not heard what had happened to the two girls, and had they done so it would have made little difference. It was winter, and before they had done there was no food left in the castle of Breteuil, and no honour. Its lady they had stripped of everything but her shift. When night came they watched still, jeering while Juliana de Breteuil clambered in some manner down the rain-soaked outer walls, her single garment pulled up by jutting stones and wind to reveal her much-invaded nakedness. They laughed loudly as she plunged into the cold and filthy moat, and swam across. Bedraggled like a half-drowned rat, and almost crazed, she was allowed at last to join her husband at Pacy. It was the end of them and they were no more heard of except as a reason for coarse men's laughter.

The king congratulated himself on his justice here, as in England. He had punished those who merited punishment, rebels, thieves, highway robbers, false moneyers, abusers of power. He was a good king of England and better duke of Normandy. He would be rewarded by God.

Had he known, God was preparing the utmost retribution. The mutilated girls in their convent heard of it in proper course, smiling beneath the drawn-down veils they must always wear lest the sight of them disgust the other inmates.

If matters remained a trifle disturbed in Normandy, England knew godly governance. The high moral character of Henry's court was evidenced by the presence of the Beaumont boys, namely the de Meulan twins and their brother Hugh, who had been reft from their wanton mother and detained in Henry's care. Unfortunately Waleran tended to stray and to prefer the company of his stepfather Earl Warren and the increasing second family at Lewes. Otherwise, apart from the lack of the queen's presence, which would have given everything an air of total legality, there was no doubt who ruled or who would next rule. There had been a time when a king's successor could not be a child or a weakling, and a strong bastard son might be preferred by his subjects instead. That could not happen now. Henry glanced with affection at his eldest, Robert of Caen, who would have made a good king but would never be one; and at Robert's half-brothers Richard, Reginald, Henry and Gilbert. There were fewer sons than daughters, but by now most of those last were provided for, in Man, Galloway, Brittany, the Isles and Scotland, not to mention various Norman bridegrooms. Henry had provided handsome dowries and, except for Juliana, could not reproach himself: and Juliana's fate had been nobody's fault but her own.

As regarded the legitimate issue, the marriage of England's heir had taken place, though little Matilda of Anjou was too young for it to be consummated quite yet. The state of other things, including that of the church in England, simmered civilly. It was unforgotten that Henry and the pope had met that time at Gisors to discuss that very matter, with an accompanying train of cardinals who had admired, even then, young Robert de Beaumont the Hunchback's learning and his ready grasp of Latin. In the old days this would have meant the crooked twin's undoubted entry into the church; now, it meant instead that he might well make a minister of state like his lately deceased father. He, King Henry, knew from his own experience that it was unnecessary to draw off all intelligence into church preferment. He would also have preferred greatly, still, to be able to invest bishops directly himself with the ring and staff, but perhaps that would come again in time; meantime, he had improved the form of lay government, barons no longer holding sway other than to be able to render due military service to the king; Henry's own chosen servants presided over courts and reported back to him directly and without delay. He told himself that he kept his fingers on the pulse of the kingdom as well as that of the duchy.

His Audelin he surveyed with pride. He would have liked to crown young William in his own lifetime, as was done in France; but one must proceed carefully. Coronation was not considered of importance in the north, though the Scots themselves had anointed their kings since time immemorial. That sprang, he told himself again, from the days of the Caesars, who had made themselves gods; and before that no doubt from the days of David and Saul. He, the Solomon of England, had been anointed, as priests were; the widening difference between a priest and a king had not become distinct by the time, for instance, of the youth of the unforgotten Columba, who had had royal blood and had had a banner carried before him wherever he went. There should be a narrowing once more of the two offices; this Henry hoped to achieve before he died. However all must be done with caution. Meantime, he could sit on his throne almost placidly. God was most certainly his ally, having proved it by repeated favourable events.

The king also noted idly that Earl Warren had returned to court and to attendance about himself, the scandal of the Vermandois elopement having abated.

It was the twenty-fifth of November, 1120. The Conqueror's old ship *Mora* rocked at anchor at Barfleur, having waited, with its pristine new sister *Blanche Nef*, three weeks for a favourable wind to England. On board was the king, and with him the Audelin's bride Matilda of Anjou, aged twelve. Henry's majestic presence awed her a little, and his deep booming voice nobody dared disobey. However he was in a kindly mood today, as everything lately had gone well. There was peace with King Louis after the homage by the heir, and a Welsh bishop at home had been consecrated by the primate, with a Welsh prince as sponsor, without argument.

Matilda did not know all this, and tried to free herself of the feeling of homesickness she still had for Le Mans and her family; there were Geoffrey and Hélie her two brothers, and Sybil her sister, returned mysteriously unmarried after all from France. Perhaps they would send her, Matilda, back also; there was still a delicate situation with the pope, as Sybil's consanguinity to the Clito had been the same as her own with the Audelin, whom Matilda found in any case noisy and overbearing. She could hear the shouting and laughter now as he and his friends boarded the

Blanche Nef. Wine had been broached, and when priests had come to bless the new ship and cast holy water, they had been mocked at and sent away. The captain himself was drunk. Matilda's gentle nature disliked the state of affairs, and she had come instead with the king. She knew none of her bold Angevin ancestry showed in her, as she resembled more greatly her dead mother, the heiress of Maine. Otherwise, there were terrifying stories about the counts of Anjou, who were supposed to be descended from the devil; yet her father Fulk was good-natured enough: she missed him badly.

'Let me show you this old ship, which was a gift to my father from my mother,' the king said, and shepherded the young girl towards the stern, telling her how the late Duchess Matilda, as she was then, had had this vessel built secretly as a surprise for her husband Duke William of Normandy when he set out on his great English adventure in 1066. '*Mora* means delay,' he explained. 'She was afraid he would never return; but my father returned to her often, and when she came to England after he was king, I was born to them there.' He could never refrain from bringing this to everyone's mind. His long robes whipped in the November wind as they walked the decks, the child's unripe body keeping up with his tall man's strides. They came to the stern, where a small figure of a boy stood fastened forever there in gilt bronze, blowing a horn.

'Who is that?' exclaimed Matilda in delight. He was a charming little boy, she decided, smaller than life. The king frowned quickly, then concealed it.

'That is an image of my brother, the late King William II, as a child. He was our father's favourite, and my mother knew it would please him to have the boy's likeness standing on the ship, heartening him on.' The thought was bitter as always; he himself had not yet been conceived, but even after that Rufus had remained the best-loved son. No matter now; he was no more than forgotten bones in the dark. 'Come,' he said to his son's bride, 'and see the people who are crowding to watch us depart.'

These thronged the quay, as much to see the great new White Ship begin her first sea-voyage as to say farewell to a duke they did not greatly love. Their faces gaped upwards; the sails filled with the wind. The *Mora* had her anchor hauled up, and began at once to move; it was etiquette for the king's ship to lead. The grey Channel stretched before them, tossed today into high waves. Matilda clutched her cloak about her, and listened to the drunken sounds from the *Blanche Nef*, still in port. They had refused, she thought again, to have holy water sprinkled on her, saying they had wine.

She stood, the young bride from Anjou, at the stern, watching while the great new ship began to follow. She kept one hand on the little gleaming figure of William Rufus, as if he were a friend. She had heard somewhere that he had said no king had ever drowned; otherwise, the waves were frightening. It seemed as if their ship was moving faster than the other and that they would reach England first. That was as it ought to be, no doubt, but the *Blanche Nef* was listing.

The sea-spray dampened Matilda's face and the wind blew her hair across it. Soon she thought she heard faint cries in the distance. Something was wrong. The king had gone below; ought she to disturb him? Perhaps, after all, she was imagining it, unused as she was to anything to do with the sea. However there seemed confusion in the other ship, which by now was lurching dangerously. Soon the *Nef* began to sink rapidly. The cries increased, and figures crowded on deck and a boat was being put out. It was difficult to see more for high waves and spray. Matilda picked up her skirts and ran in terror to find the king. By the time they hastened back on deck, nothing remained to be seen or heard except the howling wind, and the churning and sated sea.

*

News of the drowning of England's heir the Audelin, and his half-brother Richard and many others, did not reach land for some days. There was only one survivor, a butcher who had clung to the mast of the doomed *Blanche Nef*. It had struck a rock almost as soon as they left harbour, the captain as aforesaid being drunk. Several of the young folk, including the Audelin himself, had been saved at first in the small-boat, he having been borne there in his tutor's arms; but his half-sister whom he best loved, Matilda de la Perche, had been seen struggling in the water and had cried out to William to turn back and save her. He had ordered this, and the small-boat had capsized with extra weight of numbers by then clinging to it, so all in the end had drowned. The captain had deliberately made himself sink beneath the waves, saying he could not face the king.

Nobody dared to break the news to Henry. In the end a little page was sent. The child knelt, with a sorrowful face. He told the king his son was drowned, with all the rest; that they had not found the Audelin's body among those which were washed ashore, their faces eaten by fish. The last part of it he did not relate.

The king was silent, then said a strange thing. 'The lion's whelps shall change to the shapes of fishes.' It was a part of Merlin's prophecy, the one which had said that a lion of justice should arise in the land. He had not thought of it often, till now, in that last part.

The heir to England now was the Clito. Henry realised it early, even amid deep grief. Failing that – and despite the fact that he would never be known to smile again, he almost grimaced at the irony of it – failing that, there was his eldest sister's son, Earl Warren. Warren would, of course, grasp the situation at once.

A sorrowing man spent Christmas almost alone in Brampton, a place in the north where few came even from Earl David's nearby palaces. With the king was Adela's eldest, Stephen's brother Theobald of Blois. Stephen himself had been one of those who leaped ashore at Barfleur as the White Ship sailed, foreseeing danger.

The young man could say little to comfort the older one now, who sat privately doubting the sobriety of the captain, silent and mourning, the tears running down his furrowed cheeks. The king looked far older, since the news had come, than his fifty-two years. Had his nephew known, the iron will had begun to assert itself, already, while weeping for his drowned son. He must marry again without delay, and make another son while he could. All was not lost while he lived, and ruled two lands still.

PART III

1

THE WHITE SHIP had foundered exactly a month before Christmas. By Twelfth-night the king had arranged to marry again. His young bride – she was eighteen – was of impeccable lineage, the duke of Louvain's daughter, a descendant of Charlemagne and niece to the pope. She was known as the Fair Maid of Brabant. She was pious and gentle, had no humour, and was a noted embroideress. Her name was Adeliza.

Henry, interested mostly in Adeliza's fertility, although a second pious and high-born queen would do no harm, arranged for her to be met at Dover, but did not go in person. The Fair Maid was thereafter escorted to Windsor on the Feast of the Purification, and married to the king at once.

Henry found that she knew no English, and had to explain to her through a chaplain that as the archbishop of Canterbury was indisposed, her hallowing could not take place till next day. Meantime, they were bedded.

Here Henry encountered his first defeat. The sight of a pretty young woman lying in his bed should have presented no difficulties. The charms of Adeliza had not been fully manifest beneath the enveloping cloak she wore on arrival, which was nunlike and copious, covering her head in its close hood and revealing only candid eyes and a rosebud mouth. Now, all was in order except that he himself, for the first time in his adult life, could not sustain an erection.

He grunted some excuse, rolled off her and later tried again. It was useless; the shock of the Audelin's death and his own cloistered existence of late months had no doubt made an old man of him. He slept, and snored; Henry's snores were famous as allowing no one nearby in his palaces to get to sleep. Queen Adeliza lay wakeful, tired after her journey but prevented from rest. Being pious, she said her prayers till dawn, some of them on behalf of the king. She was sorry for him; he had lost his son and wanted another, and she had come prepared to do her duty. However not enough had happened, and tomorrow she was to be crowned.

A crumpled, bewildered and sleepless young creature was conveyed next day before a recovered archbishop – Ralph the primate had had an attack of bile, no more – and, in the current expression, hallowed to queen. Henry watched the setting of Mald's light crown on his new consort's head with pride. He would try again tonight. It was incredible that he, the father of so many out of wedlock, should not contrive one more within it.

He tried; but the majestic heavings that resulted in the nuptial bed were to no purpose. Adeliza's fate for the next fourteen years was to endure them; but this troubled her less than a second night devoid of sleep. This state of things continued, and she did not like, or know how to ask, the king at least partly to occupy a separate bed. In the end, after a week of seeing her young mistress haggard and with red-rimmed eyes, her waiting-woman told the chaplain and the chaplain told the king. In Latin it sounded less undignified. Henry was instantly remorseful; henceforth he would sleep in a different bed, having first visited his queen. This proved more successful in the liveliness of the obedient bride by day; but matters regarding the marriage itself did not improve. The king greatly regretted having wasted so much seed on too many mistresses; he tried to revive matters with hot cloths, nostrums from his physicians, even advice from his son Robert, who was the only one with whom he could discuss such things now Robert de Meulan was dead. Nothing availed, and at last he burst out crying on his young queen's bare breast; the hot tears bathed her flesh.

She was pitiful, and took the grey head in her arms. '*Unglücklich Mann*,' she said softly. Perhaps it would come. She held him for a time as though he had been the child they were unable to conceive. Next day she went to her prie-dieu and prayed for recovery for him, but it did not happen.

She, herself being a foreigner and used to obey in a different fashion from Mald in her early days at Wilton, could be of less help than her predecessor in signing writs and dealing with other matters in the king's absence. She accompanied Henry quietly on his various journeyings, several times to Normandy. She was given to sewing altar-cloths rather than visiting the poor; in any case, the Good Queen had left all such matters in accustomed hands and her hospitals continued to exercise their prescribed mercy and healing. Adeliza visited Mald's tomb at Westminster, saw the many candles burning, and promised that when the king died she would see to it that his burned also, at his head and his feet. More she could not do, and she came out into the daylight to a rabble of folk who stared at this young foreign woman who seemed to be barren; the marriage to the king was several months old by now.

One who had watched Adeliza crowned, seeing her meek white neck bent for the hallowing, was a young man named William de Albini, reputed to be the strongest man in England. Later legends were to gather about him regarding this strength, and the unrequited passion he inspired in the queen of France. Meantime he had begun as a butler in Snettisham, noted soon by the king for his abilities, with enough promotion thereby to enable him to live later on at Arundel. He was struck by the beauty of the young queen, and gently attached himself to her with a devotion which remained entirely innocent. Albini knew a little German, and was able to elicit from Adeliza that she had seen the king's daughter, the empress, at her court abroad. 'She is very handsome,' the queen managed to say by then in English. She returned to her embroidery and Albini to his manly avocations, which did not include the legend later attached to him, that the French queen, enraged that he would not return her love, had shut him in a cave with a roaring lion, whose tongue Albini had duly torn out by reaching down its throat. The only lions readily available were those at Windsor and Woodstock, where the porcupine had long since joined them and was to be seen expanding its grey-black quills when so inclined.

The Audelin's own young widowed bride had been reclaimed by her father, though Henry kept the dowry. Matilda of Anjou in any case announced that she had no wish to marry again and would enter a convent. This decision was taken by all as signifying her devotion to the memory of the young drowned prince her husband, whom in fact she had not greatly liked and had found somewhat arrogant. The peace of the cloister seemed preferable to another such, or perhaps worse. Matilda went off to Fontevrault, where in the end she became abbess. Her sister Sybil regretted losing the Clito, who by now was married instead to a kinswoman of the king of France, having become despite everything the heir to England and Normandy. He had been as beautiful as an angel, although it was rumoured that he kept a mistress. Time passed, and another marriage was arranged for Sybil; she herself had no wish to become a nun.

Towards the end of the following year yet another young man came to court. He was a son, got beneath the rose, of old Alan

Fergeant of Brittany, and called himself Brien FitzCount. He seemed agreeable and loyal, willing to serve in any capacity, and had narrowly missed an excursion of the king's into Wales to deal with the rebellious sons of Cadogan, one of whom had, earlier, briefly carried off Nest. However Nest by now was not sought out by the king: Henry in fact blamed her for the squandering of his manhood. He continued as a model husband to all intents except one, and had himself crowned, with Adeliza, once more that year at Westminster. He had moreover founded a great new abbey at Reading, where he expected to be buried. There was no harm in making arrangements for the prospect which increasingly, and unavoidably, confronted him.

The thought of death pursued Henry all of that year, especially as his daughter Sybilla, the childless queen of Scots, died alone on an island in Loch Tay. Her spouse Alexander the Fierce was said to be ailing, in the way his brother Edgar had ailed; there was a delicacy in that family. If Earl David survived, which seemed probable from his present state of health, he would be king of Scotland; and his queen-to-be Maud owed her inheritance to one's own goodwill, the broad lands of Northampton and Huntingdon. Peace was, therefore, likely on the northern border even if he himself should die; but who in that case would be king of England? Earl Warren had begun to sign himself de Warenne again, as if to flaunt his Vermandois marriage with its probable advantages in Normandy; and his stepson Waleran would support him in any attempt there. It was not however politic to imprison either of them; on the surface, they were his supporters, and young Robert, the hunchback twin, was loyal.

The king, not for the first time, remembered his daughter in Germany, but her marriage to the emperor had bred no children. Henry decided to see her, and sent a request to her to visit him in

England. He waited, but Aaliz-Matilda did not come; and instead sent word that she had set out, but that the count of Flanders had refused to let her pass through his lands. This enraged Henry; it seemed like an open acknowledgement of his late weakness in having no heir to succeed. He was still trying to consummate his marriage to his patient and helpful young queen, but it did not seem now as if a descendant of Charlemagne would sit on the throne of England. Henry reflected wryly that that same emperor, whose known affection for his daughters had at the time been rumoured to exceed the bounds of propriety, had declined to send one of them as a bride to a king of the then divided England, it was said because the great Charles preferred to sleep with her himself. Henry hastened to disclaim any such intention with regard to Aaliz-Matilda even had it been possible for him, but he had for some time wondered why her marriage, which had been officially celebrated seven years ago now, had resulted in no heirs. Altogether the future itself seemed barren; and meantime the king ennobled Robert of Caen, his eldest illegitimate son, deservedly bestowing on him the earldom of Gloucester. At worst, Henry decided, Robert would hold the kingdom together in the event of his own death, though the English would no longer accept a bastard as their king.

The claim of Adela's sons the king had not forgotten, for he forgot nothing; but it was less likely to cause trouble than the possible claim of de Warenne in the event. Theobald of Blois was taken up with his lands abroad, Henry was a churchman, William lacking in wits, and there remained Stephen, whose future promised too idle and prosperous a life for him, as he would become, to need altering; he had recently married Mary's daughter, the young heiress of Boulogne.

It was a happy bridal, and had lifted even Henry out of his

gloomy thoughts. Stephen himself was as handsome as a bridegroom could be, and Matilda of Boulogne was the daughter of Mald's only sister, bringing with her a handsome dowry in wool and trade with the great overseas port. That she was a descendant of the Knight of the Swan was evident in a certain devoted courage to be seen in her face; difficult to describe, as she was not beautiful and, like her mother, inclined to plumpness. Her hair hung no longer than shoulder-length, and her dress, for so rich a young woman, was plain like the Louvain queen's. No doubt she had been reared piously; her father Count Eustace had, on her marriage, conveyed all his possessions to her – she was the only child – and had taken vows thereafter as a monk at Cluny. Stephen and his Matilda were left to enjoy their possessions abroad, the title of Mortain itself having been given Stephen by the king following the blinding of its original owner after Tenchebrai. No, Stephen of Mortain, count of Boulogne, had every reason to be loyal to the reigning house in England, especially as the Londoners doted on his bride, remembering her aunt the Good Queen and the probability that they themselves would grow prosperous over the years with the trade she brought. As for Stephen, he was solemnly occupied with building a monastery for the unrewarding Cistercians, who required solitude, in Lancashire; Henry had seen it when he himself rode north, just before King Alexander died, to Durham among other places, where the Scots monarch, as a prince then, had given the suit of Turkish armour and the Arab horse long ago. The singular axe-carvings of the pillars occupied King Henry more; he had not attempted such workmanship at Reading.

He prayed at the resplendent tomb of St Cuthbert, asking that he might be sent an heir. The saint was said never to refuse aid; but meantime it did not come. Perhaps the fact that old Ranulf Flambard still survived to enjoy the revenues of his bishopric was unwelcome to the guardian of the ancient faith.

*

Events in Flanders continued to engage Henry. After the insult of refusing to allow his daughter passage, the subsequent count, known as Charles the Good, was quite independently murdered. Eventually governance was to be given to none other than the young Clito, whose upbringing had certainly made him unsuited to rule so stiff-necked a people; they made good mercenaries, artisans and settlers, but were not high-born. That the Clito should be given an independence at all was intolerable. One of the few times when the king was angry with his gentle Adeliza was when she suggested, knowing his perturbation over the lack of an heir, that he invite his brother's son to come to England. It was the obvious answer, at any rate to her straightforward mind; he quelled her.

'Mind your woman's tasks, and leave affairs of state to those who understand them.'

Nevertheless had he had a conscience, it would have reproached him; he recalled the time when Louis the Fat, Fulk of Anjou and Baldwin of Flanders had united to try to destroy him, not only in Normandy but in England, having decided that Curthose's son should wear the Conqueror's crown. He, Henry, had countered by making an alliance with Fulk, cozening the pope with fair words at Gisors – how long ago that seemed! – and wrecking the marriage arranged about then between the Clito and Fulk's daughter Sybil. That had taken much gold and many presents, and involved the convenient old cause of consanguinity. The replete pontiff – his successor might not have been as easy – had been heard to breathe, by the end of all the banquets, that nothing was more just than the king of England's cause.

Meantime, with the Audelin's homage to Louis himself, any discontented Normans had known themselves beaten and had turned to the Audelin again; the memory seared his father. It had seemed like checkmate for the Clito, who at that time had besought that his own father be given him and promised to go with old Curthose to Jerusalem and never to trouble the king of England more.

Now, matters were different; the Clito ruled in Flanders, Curthose was still alive in his English jail, and Henry had no heir.

By now, also, Anjou was hostile again. Count Fulk had lately sent envoys to demand the return of young Matilda's dowry. Henry refused – the girl was after all a nun in his territories – and the envoys had returned to Angers breathing war. If was as if heaven, if heaven could favour the devil's descent of Anjou, conspired against him, the king, in all directions.

He did his best to placate heaven. He had already ordered a light to burn perpetually over Mald's tomb at Westminster, paying a halfpenny a day out of his London rents. It was Adeliza who told him, in the English she was beginning to learn, that many more candles were burning there, placed by the common people who had never forgotten the Good Queen. Would they accept the rule of the Good Queen's daughter? It would mean, no doubt, bringing in aid from her husband and Germany; but after all England had once been ruled successfully by the Danes. Times changed, and he himself must look ahead, beyond his own grave; he could not live for ever, though he had as yet no malady other than sadness and impotence.

Nevertheless it was the emperor who died, in the year after Alexander of Scots. The death had evidently taken place at Utrecht in early May. There was no question now but that Aaliz-Matilda must come home, and be married this time to a husband who would father children on her. Henry knew already whom he had daringly selected; the young brother of Matilda of Anjou. Such a marriage would serve two purposes; to keep Anjou and Maine allied to Normandy and himself, and to give heirs to England.

However he kept silent meantime on the matter, knowing the Angevins were considered rough and bestial by the English, even in the way they ate. Also, Count Fulk must be again won over.

He sent a demand, once more, for the empress to come home, this time by sea.

PART IV

1

A BARGE WAS travelling in state along the winding Seine towards Rouen, with a handsome woman of twenty-five seated centrally on a dais on deck. Her widow's veil stirred lightly in the summer breeze, but was held firmly in place by a gleaming jewelled crown. The empress herself, Kaiserin Mathilde, sat placidly, confident that, this time, all would be as she had ordered it on the journey. The insolence of the late count of Flanders in refusing oneself passage had not been given the opportunity to repeat itself on this occasion; one had avoided the territory of his successor by arriving directly at Le Havre. The whole business had in any case stemmed from the enmity of the king of France towards one's father, the king of England, and need be of no further concern.

Mathilde herself was well used to govern. Her late husband the emperor had left her in charge of his armies and councils in Italy, returning by himself across the mountains, when she was hardly more than sixteen. She had been his helpmeet from the beginning; their relationship had been that of a trusting father and daughter. She mourned Henry V sincerely, but trusted that her own acknowledged control of matters had ensured her lasting respect, not only in Germany but elsewhere. She had travelled widely with the emperor in his lifetime; she could remember, while the river glided past now, the days of their shared glory, when she had ridden by his side into Rome to see him crowned. Earlier they had inhabited the palace of the doges in Venice, above waters wider by far than this celebrated Seine. Mathilde could remember the lagoons and floating islands, vanishing into Adriatic mist. She had seen snow also, at such places as Canossa in the Italian Alps, where the emperor's father had been humiliated by kneeling four days and nights in the snow, outside the castle, a penance which proved in its nature temporary. They themselves had however visited the place in April, the present pope no longer being as troublesome as Gregory VII, and the mountains covered, in hidden places, with the blue blaze of gentians, to her amazement. She had run about, still young then, and gathered the trumpet-like flowers in her hands; the emperor had smiled, watching her. 'You are a child,' he had said, 'my own dear child,' and the sight of the flowers had shaken him out of his gloomy moods, which were frequent. She knew that the remembrance of his father's death troubled him always, blaming himself as he did. 'He fell on my neck, and embraced me; and I left him to die.' It was for that reason that Henry V had privately failed to consummate their marriage, although officially they had been bedded after a great ceremony when Mathilde herself was fourteen. Lying in the dark the emperor had caressed her, stroking her limbs and hair, then had taken her hand and kissed it respectfully. 'You are a great king's daughter,' he had said, 'and I honour you as my wife; but I am a guilty man and will not presume to touch you.' He had never done so, though they had continued to share the same bed. It had never been asked, by the respectful Germans, why she bore no children; but she suspected that her father the king, having sent for her, would enquire now. They had not wanted her to leave, her loyal Germans; they had begged her to stay and rule them, the alternative ruler being unsatisfactory: had even sent envoys to the king her father, but to no purpose. The emperor had had considerable trouble with his kinsmen in his lifetime: there might be more, lacking her, now. There was also the mystery surrounding his death a year ago.

Mathilde firmed her lips, remembering. Word had reached her that her husband had died at Utrecht. She had formerly wakened one morning to find him gone from her bed, and his gown and shoes still lying beside it. She had stayed where she was, then the news of the death had come; also that the emperor had already been buried at Speyer. Why had there been such haste? She had not been consulted as to the requiem rites, or given time to attend them. The regalia, or most of it, her husband had left with her, and it had been taken from her by a trick. Nevertheless she had kept the crown, and wore it now. That, and certain jewels, would be safe in England when they crossed over together, she and the king her father.

A greater jewel confronted the empress where she sat now, and she had spent much of the voyage regarding it, and praying before it. It was the hand of St James, housed in its reliquary; obtained by her on a recent pilgrimage she had made to Compostela. It was to be a gift for King Henry's new abbey of Reading. There was no question but that he would welcome such a gift; the quality of his welcome to herself was however shrouded in many questions. What did he want of her? There was no doubt that her visit was in some way connected with her brother the Audelin's drowning six years ago, and the childlessness of her father's new queen since: a pity. Mathilde recalled seeing the young girl at the emperor's court with her father, the duke of Louvain, and had approved Adeliza's modesty. Nevertheless for herself to inherit England, in her widowed state, would mean that the rival heir, the Clito, and his still surviving father must be rendered harmless. She would recommend stricter imprisonment for Robert Curthose, whom she did not remember; one understood that he had gazed on her at her birth. The question of ridding oneself of the Clito must follow before his recent marriage to the king of France's kinswoman could produce heirs. No doubt her father wanted to consult her on both these points. She would give him her considered advice.

Her expression was calm, surveying the withered hand in its crystal. The holy body had arrived in Spain long ago by a miracle, aided by a storm and shipwreck. Perhaps the drowning of the Audelin had been a similar act of God, though one would not of course say so; from all she remembered and had heard, William had been somewhat arrogant. She herself, on the other hand, was known in Germany as Mathilde the Good, like her mother; even, for having restored certain monks their tithes and deciding in favour of a bishop at a court hearing, Mathilde the Pious. Ruling England would be similar to ruling Germany; one had to be firm, and would then be obeyed.

She bowed regally to the common people, who now that the capital was almost reached had come out to throng the river's banks to see her pass. The churchmen who accompanied her – her father had sent a cluster of bishops to meet her at Le Havre – scattered blessings with raised hands, their low mitres gleaming. It was natural that the people here welcomed her, Mathilde was thinking; her presence meant solid aid, Germany against France. It was certain that her husband's successor would do as she bade him, even from abroad. She had ensured this before leaving.

The tall gleaming crucifix was raised as the quay approached, the relic reverently given into her hands as she rose to disembark. Crowned, glistening, unperturbed, the empress moved with dignity to the gangplank, leaving the barge rocking on the Seine and reflecting Rouen's clustered houses.

A corpulent old man with grey hair waited, surrounded by nobles; but for his crown, Mathilde would not have known her father. They embraced, after giving into King Henry's hands the hand that had once touched Christ's; then the empress kissed Queen Adeliza, who waited quietly a little behind; and a tall man she remembered, who was her half-brother Robert, earl of Gloucester now; and lastly a bright-haired younger knight, who was evidently her cousin, Stephen of Blois and Mortain. She understood that he had been married lately.

They progressed to the castle, the grace-cup, and later on the banquet. Mathilde found that she was hungry, having taken nothing since a collation on the voyage. It was not till after she had refreshed herself and eaten that the king sent for her to come to his private chamber, leaving minstrels to entertain the company. The sound of their lays came up to her, muffled as they were by the curtain pulled across the doorway.

'Now that the Rouennais have seen you for themselves, we will return to England shortly. I would have them swear to obey you there as Lady of the English, in oaths that cannot be broken after my death. Before that, to provide heirs, you must marry.' He had not asked her about the emperor. Mathilde clenched her fists, feeling her crown suddenly heavy. To marry? She had not, oddly, considered it; and knew the reason. Her husband the emperor had often confided in her that, to expiate his guilt, he desired greatly to go as a pilgrim, with grey gown and staff, alone to the Holy Land. It was not impossible that this had happened. His death and requiem had been unnecessarily mysterious; who lay in the coffin at Speyer? She knew that this had always hidden itself deep in her mind. She heard herself answer coolly.

'I have ruled my late husband's realms well enough, and commanded his armies. It is not agreeable to me to marry again. The English themselves have not always elected the sons of their kings.'

'The English have never been ruled by a woman, and would by

no means agree to it. You must have a husband, and I have one for you; as yet, he is somewhat young.' He did not easily mention Geoffrey of Anjou, or that the lad was still scarcely fourteen: but it had to be done. The sight of his daughter, grown to stately womanhood, overawed Henry despite himself; and that condition of things he would by no means permit. He heard her voice tremble suddenly, and was reassured; he could master her. Feigning fatigue, he removed his crown and laid it aside, bidding Mathilde do the same. 'These are heavy,' he admitted. Lacking it, she saw that his hair was thinning as well as grey: unlike Adeliza, she had no compassion. She remembered the younger men with whom she had sat at the high table; handsome Stephen of Blois, count of Mortain and, by marriage, of Boulogne, who had charmed her by his looks, ready smile and easy entertaining talk, different from her heavy obedient Germans at the imperial court; and the other, Brien FitzCount, who regarded her already with a dog's loyalty, and was by now married to one of the king's everlasting illegitimate Matildas, with her dowry of Wallingford. Both of these agreeable men were married; and she, their Lady, was expected to make do with some other.

'Who is to be my husband, as you have decided it?' She questioned within herself whether or not to tell him about the emperor's disappearance, barefoot and clad in wool, from her bed last year. It was possible that, did she do so, the king would select some other to inherit England; and already the prospect of becoming Lady of the English satisfied Mathilde. She fingered her crown, which lay shining now in her lap. It bore gems from the time of St Kunigünde, and from the earlier time of Charlemagne. When the king told her that her bridegroom was to be the young count of Anjou, she bit her lips in rage.

'The Angevins are savages,' she said. 'Their manners disgust the English; I know as much from my chaplains, who have travelled in the region.' There had been an interesting connection there with the old Columban church, which her grandmother Queen Margaret had suppressed in Scotland, but which had sent out brave missionaries to all parts of Germany, including the odd geographer Virgil at Salzburg who insisted that the world must be round. To entertain such thoughts was, at present, irrelevant. But Anjou! Perhaps she could at least delay such a marriage; her father might after all be dead before it came about.

'The alliance is necessary to secure the frontiers of Normandy, which your son will also inherit,' remarked the king smoothly.

St James's hand gleamed within its crystal, having witnessed many things.

The empress found, on return to England, that all such things as she recalled from childhood seemed smaller; after the great tracts of Germany and the dizzy heights of the Alps, it was a little rich land, a land both to love and to desire. The only things she could recall which had been smaller in Germany by contrast were the tiny Rhine herons, diving with diligence along the broad river for fish. She had watched them long ago while voyaging to Bingen, and had contrasted them then with the huge and majestic creatures which would stand one-legged by English water, waiting, waiting; and then flash suddenly down, bringing up a gleaming fish and swallowing, or else taking it to a tree-nest in enormous flapping flight. There were herons and hawks, and in Germany, as here, she had liked to ride out with a falcon, keeping the due meat from it to cause it to return the more swiftly, her skirts kilted up to ride like a man in the saddle, in the way they frowned on here; but she was accustomed to it now and would not give it up. She rode out thus with the king and her half-brother at Woodstock, in the park, to see the animals and the lodges Henry had built for them and their keepers. The king, who had hoisted his unwieldy body into the saddle with surprising ease, told her the tale of how the bishop of Lincoln, who had been riding exactly here, with the bishop of Salisbury on the king's other side, to view the same lodges last year, had suddenly dropped dead from his horse. 'It was useless to carry him back,' the king said, 'as he was already dead.'

She put in swiftly 'And, my lord, had it been the bishop of Salisbury who had dropped dead, he would have left a prisoner the more easily to be freed. Bishop Roger is an old man now; should aught befall him in such ways, his mistress and his son keep the castle of Devizes, and their hands are not strong; followers of my uncle Robert Curthose might well free him before you as much as learned of the good bishop's death.'

'Devizes is a strong castle,' said the king tetchily; he found his daughter masterful after gentle Adeliza and the empress's own half-remembered mother. Robert of Gloucester, who had overheard, put in eagerly that his sister was right.

'Give him to me, and I will ward him safe in Cardiff,' he said. 'It is the more urgent that he should be kept close now his son rules in Flanders, and might send him sudden aid.'

'Well, we will see,' grumbled the king, but he arranged the matter; and at the same time, knowing wicked old Ranulf Flambard had not been well on the occasion of his own visit to Durham, arranged for quick messengers to take and bring in the profits of that see as soon as news should come of Ranulf's death. Meanwhile, to still the doubts of those who thought he had no care for the church, he had installed a learned personage named Gilbert the Universal as bishop of London, he having been formerly master of the schools at Nevers.

By then, the empress knew that she craved two things equally: England, her rightful inheritance, shortly soon in nature to be her own; and, for the first time, a man's bright-haired body in her bed; that of no other than Stephen of Blois, count of Mortain and

Boulogne, her cousin, equal in rank as far as any man could be, and with his own share, like hers, of the blood of the Conqueror. They could have made fine sons together; it was a pity about the dull little wife; everything had happened too soon or too late, by a mere matter of months. One understood that the wool heiress was pregnant. Perhaps she would die in childbirth. If Stephen could be her own husband he would defend the borders of Normandy against all comers, including no doubt the wretched boy from Anjou. Even her father must see that. It was necessary to have patience, like the waiting herons; and to make her own plans as far as she might.

She watched Stephen's bright head bend in homage to her as Lady of the English, after a slight altercation between Stephen himself and Robert of Gloucester, who claimed the first vassalage after her maternal uncle David of Scotland, an anointed king. David had knelt first; then Stephen, in the age-old act of homage, placing his hands between hers; his touch made her blood run warm and swiftly despite the cold day. Others, followed, the prelates and the nobility of England and Normandy, swearing to be loyal to her for both realms. The ceremony seemed unending, and it was January weather, with everyone clad for preference in furs. Mathilde was aware of no particular emotion; they were after all conceding what was hers by right. One obstacle was the Clito, whose existence must be remembered; there had been a recent plot to kill him, but he had been warned in time by his mistress, who had the habit, on his visits, of washing and combing his long hair. Why did she think of that now, when one after the other great noble knelt in homage? King David her uncle would be faithful whatever befell; so would Brien FitzCount, and her half-brother Robert of Gloucester. However nothing in any case should go amiss. She would control matters, as she had done with the armies in Italy. Monsters such as

Robert of Bellême lay in prison in chains; these men today were her father's, and would be hers in time.

The king watched, pleased with his daughter's demeanour; she had looks and dignity, if only she would behave somewhat less like a man. For some reason he found himself remembering his brother Rufus, who had built this hall and then said it was not grand enough to be anything but a place in which to dine. It was on a par with the boast he had made about building a bridge of boats over to Ireland from Wales. It had not happened; and Henry himself had not troubled with Ireland, there was enough to deal with elsewhere for the time. Perhaps the sons of the empress and Geoffrey of Anjou would in their day venture across the narrow strait. Henry kept the matter of Geoffrey to himself, for the good reason that the barons had sworn fealty only on the understanding that they should have some say in the empress's marriage, and that it should not take place out of England. It was a pity, in a way, that Stephen of Mortain, whom the king greatly liked, was unavailable by reason of the recent Boulogne marriage; and his other brother was a churchman, and Theobald and William would not do. The world, and the personages in it, passed by in the king's mind like a pageant; he had never been one of its participants since the death of his son. By now, that was seven years ago, and he, the king, had never smiled since.

'Send me the count of Mortain. We would be private.'

Queen Adeliza, in whose apartments the empress was staying, dared not question her imperious stepdaughter; but was it entirely proper to receive the count alone? She did not disobey, however, and went to have Stephen fetched, ensuring privacy in the usual way by arranging the curtains. She made herself sit elsewhere by the light of a rush-lamp, trying to see her present task of an embroidered altar-cloth, but the light was not strong enough, and she did not want to eavesdrop. Against a wall lay one of the late Queen Mald's lutes, which she had been wont to play, one understood, very well. Adeliza took it up, smoothed the ribbons and strummed sad little notes, chiefly to make it clear that she was not listening to whatever might chance beyond the curtain. It was not, of course, as she admitted, her concern, and certainly best not mentioned to the king.

'You know that I love you.'

She said the words without preamble, like one used at once to receiving what she asked. He stood before her with the light from the candles glinting on his hair; he had put off his formal robes and wore a plain woollen tunic, warm enough with the braziers lit everywhere. She could not see his face, which was against such light as there was. 'Look at me,' she said, and put her hands one either side his head, pulling him to her.

Count Stephen was a good-natured young man, directed in youth by his masterful mother and still inclined to obey commands from women without question. Moreover he was the soul of courtesy and would never disoblige anyone if it could be avoided. He was somewhat in awe of his cousin the empress, and remembered the homage earlier: yet she stood now as if in supplication, and he heard her speak in a low voice.

'They married me as a child to an old man, who was good to me, but acted as my father,' she said. 'Now they will wed me to a callow boy; had you been free, we could have married one another. Must I destroy my own maidenhead with a sharp stone as the pagans do, in order that this boy I am to marry may not mock me? Am I so ugly? Will not you lie with me, as I ask?'

'You are not ugly,' he heard himself saying. She had slipped out of her robe, revealing her body. It was that of Juno; hadn't he heard of some prince who had presumed to Juno, thereafter being thrown down from heaven as a punishment? The tale must have come from his tutors, some of whom had been to the East and learned the Greek myths there. He couldn't remember the prince's name. What breasts Mathilde had! A heady scent came from her, of mingled flowers and musk. It was difficult to remember his plump little wife, of whom he was fond; but he had already been unfaithful, and why not now? Ixion, that was the prince's name.

The flame enveloped them both thereafter, rising high till it burned to ashes. She was aware of pain, then of a swift, brief glory. This was what should have been; this was, should be again. This was loving as it should take place between a man and his wife; his wife. Why remember that now? She summoned the magic of all her ancestresses, the beautiful and beguiling women whose blood matched the Conqueror's own in her veins; Duchess Gunnor, her daughter Emma of Normandy, the tanner's daughter Arletta of Falaise, Margaret of Scotland, Matilda of Flanders. She was all of them and herself, for this hour; years later she was to write to the man she kept by then in chains after the battle of Lincoln *You know well enough what passed between us two*. Her father had, after all, taught her to write.

It passed; and he was gone. The sounds of Adeliza's lute came humbly, even yet, from beyond the curtain.

Count Geoffrey of Anjou, aged fifteen, knelt before the altar in Rouen, hands on his poised sword in ritual fashion, undergoing his vigil before being knighted on the morrow, which was Whitsun of 1128. He shifted his lithe weight surreptitiously from one knee to the other; it was a long time till dawn. He was more at home in the saddle than on foot, and rode everywhere, known in season by the spring of yellow broom-flowers he had once thoughtlessly stuck in his cap while out hunting. Nobody had ever forgotten the sight, and the *planta genista*, which he'd dug in anywhere and everywhere for coverts for game in Anjou, had given him a name; Plantagenet.

Otherwise they called him Geoffrey Le Bel, and he knew it. He was handsome as a god, slim as a young tree, fair-haired and with cool light eyes that missed nothing. His mouth might be described as whimsical by women, or else calculating by men. Even the young girls among the Norman peasantry, crowding the roads lately to watch him ride by, had refrained from the snarled 'Guirrebecs!' his Angevins met with here by custom, and had smiled at him instead. Geoffrey had winked back; there was no pretence of devotion at the prospect of this elderly bride, king's daughter and empress or not. In fact he himself would shortly be a king's son, though he had kept silent on it till it became a fact. His widowed father, Fulk, had been chosen to marry the heiress of Jerusalem, King Baldwin's daughter Mélisende: and Baldwin was dying. There would soon be an Angevin king in the Christian kingdom carved out by the pilgrimage of a generation since, with its bloodshed and internal squabbles and treacheries and miracles and sacrifice. Geoffrey wished his father joy. They said Princess Mélisende was a bitch, though beautiful. That made two brides to subdue; one had heard also of the empress's high temper. Well, he could meet it with a slap in the face, perhaps on the bottom. She was, when all was said, descended from sea-pirates; their tombs lay behind him now; old Rollo, old Longsword. He himself had by far more varied an ancestry; one could after all achieve no greater distinction than being descended from the devil. Geoffrey shifted his weight again, and briefly recalled the demon ancestress who had flown out of the window in church at the elevation of the Host, taking two of her sons with her and leaving her cloak, and the other two, behind. That last was important, as it had founded the resulting line of ancestors with interesting names; Geoffrey Greygown, Fulk the Red, Fulk Nerra who had been four times to Jerusalem and back, and had bitten off a piece of the Holy Sepulchre with his teeth to bring home when the Saracens refused him leisure to pray there. Prayer was no doubt of little avail to that Fulk in any case, as he had burned his wife, or one of them, at the stake in her wedding dress; another forebear had strangled his. Nevertheless the race went on, and the line of Tortulf the Forester ruled to this day in Anjou, chiefly at Le Mans, otherwise at Angers in the strong castle built there. Geoffrey himself had been born in Le Mans, and had an affection for it. The burghers were happy to lend him their daughters, even now; and his father Fulk had resigned to him the title of count before departing. He, Geoffrey, was head of the family; and had no reason to love this old king of England who was to become his father-in-law after making him a knight. He could remember his sister Sybil's angry tears at being deprived of the handsome Clito by the old king's constant briberies to the pope; and the sad return of Matilda, widowed and lacking her dowry the old miser had kept. If Henry's daughter showed any of this disposition, he himself would beat her out of it.

He knew himself to be slow to anger, but that when he was angry it burned steadily like an underground fire. Matilda his sister had said the Normans, including her drowned husband, treated her like a country cousin; they had tried the same thing already with himself on arrival. He would show them otherwise, and their king, before long. Old Henry thought that by this marriage to both Anjou and Maine – Geoffrey's mother had been the heiress of the latter so that the two now were joined – Normandy would swallow up both. On the other hand – and Geoffrey assessed it in his cool and able mind – it was Anjou, in time, which would swallow up Normandy. He had already determined it. He had certain intelligence about the coming marriage of the French King's son to the little heiress of Aquitaine; that would give southern ports to France, and the Mediterranean trade. It had always been the bane of the French kings that Charles the Simple had given away his ports to old Rollo the Norman for the sake of peace; that, and the recent marriage of Henry's nephew Stephen of Blois to the Boulogne heiress had meant that England would grow rich on trade. So be it; but there were other frontiers now. He himself would by no means fall out with King Louis. He knew that, unlike his own father who could never remember names, he himself forgot nothing, neither a face nor an injury. He would watch with care which Normans and which English looked down on him, at tomorrow's ceremony and after; and in time would repay. The hand of the empress in marriage would do him no harm, and the Kaiserin Mathilde must accustom herself to being a countess, most of all on her back.

Dawn would be in an hour; Geoffrey could tell from the guttering of the candles, which had almost burned out. They would come for him then and sink him thankfully in a hot bath. He had stiffened from the long kneeling more than from the long ride yesterday, in which he had appraised the Devil's Tower they had built here on the south side of the river, for greater convenience in hunting. Otherwise, he had seen at a glance how Rouen might be taken in time of siege; he knew Vegetius' book on that subject well enough, having read it beneath the walls of a wider town waiting to be taken. The whole of life was a game of chess, and pawns must be shifted in such order as presented itself.

The bride herself had crossed the Channel in the company of her half-brother Robert of Gloucester and of Brien FitzCount, which last entertained her with the tale of how his father, old Alan Fergeant, had seen for himself the veil torn from her mother's head in girlhood in Scotland by her father King Malcolm Ceann Mór. It took one back a long way; and passed the time till they reached Rouen, and the sight of the tents set up for the week's rejoicings before her marriage.

She herself could feel no joy, only a cold sense of duty to be done. Stephen had ridden off to the north last year to busy himself with his Cistercian houses, and had left her to endure the news that his wife had borne him a son. She must thrust that episode down in her mind, as she could not forget it. The future was as blank as a piece of unmarked vellum. She watched the discreet welcome of the Rouennais, heard the chime from the tower where the last Count Bishop had lived in comfort with his wife and children in her great-great-great-grandsire's time; and allowed herself to be led into the castle and prepare to watch the knighting of Count Geoffrey, early next day. She was told that he was handsome, rode well, and was a passionate hunter; that might, after all, be one thing in common between them.

They had sunk young Count Geoffrey into a bath fragrant with herbs, dispelling his night's stiffness. They then put on his body a shirt of finer linen than he had yet worn in his life. Its comfort was more to him than the grandeur which followed; the velvet cap and black surcoat with leopards – a pard, he knew, had to do with a lioness, and the lion punished her when spots showed – to the great enamelled and jewelled chain, of a richness he had not before experienced, across his shoulders.

When he was ready, they led him into the presence of the king.

Geoffrey of Anjou regarded his future father-in-law, summing him up as he would have done any man; he himself was not a respecter of persons. He had no illusions in any case; this man was known to have worn himself out with lecheries to an extent which made it impossible for him to get a second heir. The heavy flesh beneath his eyes set off a grey face with lines between nose and mouth, the face of a man without scruple; hard, able, close-fisted, though today's ceremony certainly spared no expense. The king had stoutened notably over the years, bearing a likeness in that and other ways to his father the Conqueror, except that the Conqueror had been a faithful husband. Henry's booming voice welcomed the young count, and bade him kneel to receive the sword of knighthood, while the assembled nobility watched closely.

Geoffrey, once made a knight, showed them all what he could achieve in the feat of leaping into the saddle unaided, his rich gear gleaming. The king thought privately that he had never seen so handsome a sight. It would take a difficult woman not to be pleased with the young count of Anjou, despite the difference in their ages. Nevertheless Mathilde showed no pleasure. The king recited slowly, to her hard unchanging face, the prophecy of Merlin which promised a lion's whelp.

After the feasting was over he lay alone, and in his mind there floated up more of Merlin. There was a verse he did not fully understand even yet: it was no doubt for the future.

Drop must a Sagittary from the skies,
But against him an Eaglet shall arise,
That in the Morian mountains built her nest,
And against that celestial sign contest.
She failing, will a lion's whelp appear,
Whose roar shall make the centaur quake with fear,
And when the two-shaped monster shall be tamed,
By gentle means, the whelp shall be reclaimed;
And when the iron brood in the land shall fail,
The blood of the white dragon must prevail.

The blood of the white dragon must mean, he thought, the Saxon inheritance, which came once again through this boy from Anjou. His own blood, the iron brood, must fail in the nature of things; descent through a woman meant the loss of the father's name, while keeping his ancestry. This marriage was the best that could be done. The Lion of Justice remembered, with a twinge of grief, that other saying of Merlin's that his dead son had turned to the shape of fishes, which had devoured him. The king closed his eyes, so that the tears seeped down between the lids, then fell to his snoring sleep and the dreadful dreams that often came, mercifully forgotten on waking.

The marriage ceremony itself took place at Le Mans. After the week's feastings and trials of knightly strength among the assembled tents at Rouen, and the farewells said, it was evening by the time they reached the little town, with its wooden houses newly erected after the last burning: these had been frequent. The bride looked down her nose; it was a mean place when one remembered earlier glories; the palace of the doges, the German imperial strongholds, England itself, with Westminster and Windsor, where the king's new buildings rose handsomely. The people in the streets here cheered and shouted in their rough dialect, taking more heed of the count than herself; the women blew kisses to him, and crowded to try to seize his bridle and finger his new knightly grandeur. Again and again there was shouted a word she did not understand; Plantagenet, Plantagenet. As something to say to him, she asked her husband what it meant.

'It means hope for the future,' he replied, the cool eyes assessing her. She disliked the glance, and already disliked the count; he was insolent, and she wondered if it would be possible at least to delay consummation of the marriage; it was unsuitable and vulgar.

However when they were bedded it was evident that he intended to take her. The people still shouted in the streets, clapping their hands in a way she disliked; it was familiar. At least tomorrow they would ride on to Angers.

'Open your legs, empress. Why else do you suppose they are singing in the streets?'

She endured what followed, loathing it. It was evident that he knew what to do. No doubt he had lain with common women, even so young; they had seemed eager enough as he passed by. The empress turned her head aside and stared at the curtain; it was grimy and plain. He finished, and turned off her at last to sleep. His breath had smelled of wine and garlic and she was glad to be rid of him. Why had her father sent her here? There had been no urgency; she was a desirable match. Stephen, Stephen; if only that had come about other than it had! She closed her eyes and tried to conjure him, seeing nothing now but the remembered brightness of his hair. She recalled he had told her that his zodiac birth-sign was Sagittarius, his jewel the topaz; a suitable colour, glowing gold. If they had conceived a child that time, there would have been no need for this distasteful marriage; even the king would have been forced to change his mind.

They rode on to Angers next day, always to the shout of 'Plantagenet! Plantagenet!' It was evident that he, rather than she, the king-duke's daughter, was the centre of attention; this in itself angered Mathilde. She sat erect, borne formally in a litter, wearing a gold circlet rather than her crown, which had been left for safe keeping at Rouen. These savages would have stolen it, no doubt, and prised out the gems. A topaz. There had been none of those in the crown. It was a semi-precious stone. Stephen, the half-hearted, had after all left her. Whatever her life was to become now, it would lack him. She must behave as if she had never yielded herself. Since that time she had grown cold and proud; she knew it, and had expected to order this boy, her husband. It seemed however as if Count Geoffrey would by no means obey orders. The crowds, which had thinned along the roads, grew heavy again as they approached Angers. She saw the castle rearing above its moat. At least there was privacy here, of a kind. Mathilde dismounted at the gateway, and walked in.

Later, again, the bed stood ready, covers turned down to reveal their fur despite the summer weather. The fur was worn; until this marriage of hers there hadn't been much money, evidently.

She had felt contempt, then suddenly was aware of creeping fear, of a kind she had never known. In the doorway, sidling between her and the curtain, was an animal she had not before seen. Its eyes regarded her as though it knew all things, and cared for nobody. It was not one of the furry bright-eyed genets found in castles to keep away mice and rats; she knew those well enough. This was a malevolent creature, that wished her ill. She slid into bed and pulled the covers about her, signalling to it to go away; but it took no heed. It was grey, a ghost, its eyes like emeralds; it writhed towards her, forever graceful, a demon. 'Get away,' she heard herself screaming. 'Go.'

She heard laughter then. Count Geoffrey entered, in his bedgown, and picked up the cat. He stroked and caressed it, rubbing its fur; it purred, turning its head to look at her with triumph. She loathed it, and him.

Count Geoffrey put the cat down. 'The castle is full of these since the time of Fulk Nerra, my ancestor who brought them home,' he said. 'In the East they are treated as gods. Her name is Mélusine, after my ancestress from hell.' He climbed into bed and the cat followed, curling itself up at the foot of the covers. 'You talk like a fool,' she said spitefully, horrified at the cat's near presence. Tomorrow, she would have it drowned. As it was, its presence made her forehead break out in beads of sweat; the renewed attentions of Count Geoffrey she let pass almost unheeded.

She did not sleep, unable to endure the cat's presence. The

count's even breathing altered as dawn came, showing at last through the chinks in the plain bed-curtains. As at a signal, he slid out of bed like an eel, and went to the privy. She heard him urinating, then he vanished to dress. Shortly a girl came to draw open the curtains. She held a plate of meat and a cup of small-ale. Mathilde turned her head away.

'I want nothing,' she said. 'Bring me water in which to wash.' She was hot and tousled after such a night spent in furs in hot weather. The cat had gone with the count. The girl left also, surreptitiously slurping the small-ale for herself outside the door. There was nothing wrong with it; that bitch had had a whole night with handsome Count Geoffrey, and hadn't seemed to like that either. He'd ridden out by himself to the hunt, or would shortly. From below came the sounds of men breaking their fast, and horns winding. When the hunt was assembled and ready to start, the young bridegroom went out to the sound of cheering.

'Plantagenet! Plantagenet!'

The empress had left her bed by then, had washed, and stood unseen by the window-slit. Several besides the wedding party had joined the hunt, neighbours evidently having come as well. Her husband – she grimaced – sat already in the saddle, a fresh-plucked sprig of yellow broom in his cap, an oriflamme. She admitted coldly that he was handsome. The horns sounded and they all rode off. Mathilde remembered that she herself was a fine huntswoman; she hadn't however been asked to go with them. No doubt a bride was supposed to keep her chamber.

The girl came back to take away the ewer and to comb the tangles out of the new countess's long hair. 'Find that cat and drown it, and any others you find,' Mathilde said. 'Do so before the hunt returns. I want none left in the castle.'

The girl trembled. 'Lady, I dursn't. The young count would beat me.'

'Well, I will beat you harder if you do not do as I bid you. See to it, you hear?' She watched the servant go. It was better to assert oneself at once; they must learn who was mistress.

She had dinner served in her chamber, not desirous of the avid eyes of the returned hunters. The cats were dead, their limp sodden bodies thrown on the dunghill. When Count Geoffrey came in, she knew that he had seen them. He came straight to her and struck her across the mouth.

'You cruel bitch,' he said. 'I loved those cats. They have been with me all my life.' For instants she saw the hurt, incredulous child he would have been had it happened in childhood; then he turned and left her. She stayed reeling against the bedpost; it was the first blow struck at her in all her life. At least she would be spared the count's company tonight, evidently; perhaps he had gone to beat, then lie with, the maidservant. No doubt the young woman would relish the experience.

2

THE KING, ENRAGED, had led his troops as far as Epernon, up against the French border. He had received intelligence that, no doubt in reprisal for his marriage of his daughter to Anjou, fat Louis was amassing aid and men for the Clito in Flanders, the young man meantime having a rebellion on his hands. He, Henry, would prevent at all costs such aid from reaching Curthose's heir. Until such time as Mathilde gave him a grandson, he was vulnerable on all fronts. King Louis himself, who a little later entertained a family tragedy akin to his own, could in such an event recoup his loss; he had many sons, and the eldest prince was riding shortly and his horse stumbled on a pig, throwing and killing him. It was not a royal way to die; the Channel's cruel waves had at least made more dignified an ending. The next prince, Louis, who was said to be devout and who had been intended for the church, stepped into the dead Philip's place without pleasure. Henry himself, fighting at bay, waited now in the shimmering sunshine, staring across at France; knowing also that the castle which had been owned by de Warenne's stepson, Waleran de Meulan, was uncomfortably near Paris itself, which was why he had seized it; and that the boy himself lay in prison, while Henry ensured that de Warenne himself was close enough about him, despite his wife's recent illness, to account for his movements.

Henry encamped at Epernon for a week; and then saw the dust of riders in the distance, bearing news. Two bishops were dead; Ranulf Flambard at last, also the archbishop of Rouen. Henry repeated the orders to seize Flambard's temporal possessions for the crown. It was a long time since the old prelate had placidly enjoyed their benefits, and longer still since he had escaped by a wine-soaked silken rope from the Tower and broken his leg. They were growing old, all of them; he himself was ageing, and tiring. The effort of a campaign was more strenuous than it used to be; but it had at least to be maintained, this show of strength.

June melted into July, and another rider came, flinging himself at the king's feet.

'Sire, the Clito is dead. He seized the spear-head of a common foot-soldier who disobeyed him, and his hand was wounded, and the wound grew fevered. He was dead within five days. I have ridden day and night.'

Henry ordered him to be given a reward, and wine. Then he said 'Someone must tell the boy's father.' He felt no emotion. God still favoured him.

It appeared that Curthose already knew. In his prison at Cardiff, he had had a dream; in it, a spear wounded him in the right arm. He awoke crying bitterly 'My son is dead! My son is dead!' Nobody could account for this, but it had happened.

Now there were no rivals to Mathilde, and the sons she ought to bear. The king waited for word of her quickening, but it did not come. What if she were barren? What then?

By the middle of July, he had gone back to England. It was as if he could not bear to wait for tidings which did not arrive. An enemy of the Clito's had meantime annexed Flanders, and Henry made haste to marry him to the discarded Sybil of Anjou, who should have married the Clito herself and had been prevented then by his own bribing of the pope.

More bishops died. Among them was Giffard of Winchester, and Henry knew whom he would put in the dead man's place; his own nephew, Adela's youngest son, Henry of Blois. Stephen's younger brother had been a posthumous child, conceived in the brief time Adela had allowed her shamefully returned husband to enjoy her embraces before sending him packing back to the Holy Land and swift death. Henry had been a quiet and scholarly child in whom his royal uncle, for whom he had been named, being born in the year after Rufus's death, would have taken a fatherly interest, except that Adela proved so competent as both father and mother to her four sons, including poor William who still retained the mind of a child, that there was no need. Unlike Stephen, Henry of Blois had escaped early from his masterful mother by becoming a monk of Cluny (Adela shortly thereafter became a Cluniac nun). The king had ensured his youngest nephew promotion when it might be done, making Henry meantime abbot of Glastonbury. Although only in his middle twenties the young man had occupied the position blamelessly, and Henry could see no objection, now the vacancy had occurred, in placing his nephew in the see of Winchester.

He spent Christmas in the town, watching with pleasure while young Bishop Henry took midnight mass. In the absence of any children of his own except for those got outside the church's blessing, Henry increasingly craved the company of his Blois relations; Stephen was always pleasant and charming, and his wife Matilda gentle and yet strong, also having done her duty now with two little sons; noisy Eustance, called after the father who had also entered Cluny on her marriage, and a fat new baby named William. It cheered the king to be with them, and he contrasted what he remembered of his daughter, not to her advantage; Mathilde had been haughty and difficult, more so than was needed. He wished she would conceive by her Angevin. If she did not, was an alternative to be found in this pleasing Stephen of Blois, already with heirs? The more the king thought of it, the more agreeable it seemed; but having assembled the baronage of England to swear fealty to Mathilde as Lady of the English, it might be somewhat troublesome to change matters now.

Meantime, he freed young Waleran de Meulan, who was sharp-witted enough to know that an eye was still being kept: also, Henry kept his castles. The gesture perhaps opened the door for negotiations with France now the Clito was a threat no longer. The Clito's father Henry ordered, at last, to be blinded. There was a risk that Curthose might take it into his head to escape if he could, cause trouble, and possibly, even at his age, get another son. Henry spared Curthose the ultimate insult of castration; after all, they were brothers. He recalled that that particular fate he reserved, with loss of the right hand, for counterfeit moneyers. He had never been addicted to it as a punishment otherwise, apart from enforcing the forest laws.

As for Curthose himself, the King's own son Robert of Gloucester kept his father informed of the otherwise unchanging lack of events at remote Cardiff. However it would be easy enough to spread a rumour, if required, that the prisoner had planned a rising on the death of his heir, with intent to escape along with a few followers, and that blinding had been considered necessary although the king had been unwilling. Nobody knew the truth one way of the other, and as time passed, Henry persuaded himself that there had been no undue outrage performed on his brother.

David of Scotland rode down that year in Lent, supposedly to investigate the case of a justiciar who was to be arraigned for high treason. The man was later proved innocent, but meantime Henry felt somewhat wary of King David's long stays at court; they happened frequently, and it was evident that England was still as much home to David Margaretson as it had been in his harried boyhood. Nevertheless by now he had rich appanages of his own, a wife with lands, a kingdom, and a healthy son and heir. Henry ordered stockfish to be served throughout Lent; that would drive the Scots king home. Even flavoured with lavender it made a dry dish, and the excuse of uncertain weather and the resulting overuse of fishponds, so that their stocks were low at this penitential season, would serve.

David, chastened, offered return hospitality at Northampton next year, when he should have completed certain improvements there. He also spoke of his plans to build several abbeys along the Border. 'I want them to make a jewelled chain to the glory of God,' he said, and Henry could not doubt his sincerity; he was, after all, Mald's brother and strong in faith, stronger than he was himself.

Otherwise the year passed tediously; a fire broke out at Ascension-tide at Rochester when the court was staying there, and everyone grabbed their gear and hastened out into the smoke-filled air with as much as they could carry until the flames were brought under control. Henry accepted the hospitality of William de Albini at Arundel thereafter, and journeyed there with Adeliza, but regretted it; he decided that their host was too assiduous to his queen, though that good young creature gave no cause, by her behaviour, for reproach. However there was no doubt that he himself was a useless husband to her, as well as being too old. Were he dead, she and Albini would make a happy pair. Henry felt misery assail him, was restless and bad tempered, and in the end sailed for Normandy in August. There, he received a letter from his daughter, delivered at Rouen within a few days; would her father meet her at the abbey of Bec, where they might talk privately?

*

The trees were already turning in September when Henry rode down from Falaise, where he had based himself, towards Bec. He had known a curious unwillingness to meet his daughter, and had made the excuse of other business now for several weeks. What had made her suggest that place, of all places? He associated it with the late Archbishop Anselm, and preferred to forget that dispute; but, before that, his father had told him tales of the obscure monastery when Henry himself was a boy, intended for a monk's calling. They hadn't made a monk of him, but he remembered the Conqueror's voice, for once spending time with the youngest son. Duke William himself had come to Bec often as a young man, in the days when he was besieging the duke of Burgundy at Brionne; and had found the great Lanfranc there. Lanfranc, afterwards made by him archbishop of Canterbury, had earlier come to Bec to seek peace from his encroaching fame as a teacher at Avranches, and had happened upon the founder, Herluin, mending the bread oven. Herluin himself had long since forsaken the world and had exchanged his knight's charger for a donkey, living as a hermit at first, then being joined by others like-minded; and so the holy place had been begun. Now, Mathilde herself was waiting for him there; no doubt she had lodged at the hospice. Why was she not with her husband? There had been silence for long from Le Mans.

The king dismounted, flung the reins to his escort and bade them wait. He then strode into the church, not having put up his sword; since the episode at Dives, and Juliana's attack, he had always gone fully armed to any assignation. However the empress was there alone, kneeling before the altar, where the coffin of Herluin the founder still rested. She turned as he entered, and rose. Henry made a formal obeisance to the tabernacle, then greeted his daughter. She was not, as he had half hoped, pregnant; in fact she had lost weight and her face was austere, as if it had been carved in stone and the excess whittled away too much by the sculptor's chisel. She looked like an abbess, accustomed to penances.

'What would you with me?' he asked her. There was nobody else in the church; it was not large enough for there to be echoes, or for their voices to be heard. He watched her eyes turned to him, with appeal in them. She wore her gold circlet and veil. He saw her strike her hands together.

'I wanted to tell you for myself that I can no longer endure my marriage. If it were not for my rights over England, I would take vows.'

'This is impossible,' he said coldly. 'The baronage have sworn fealty to you. They would not be ruled by a nun. If you desire England, you must give England heirs.'

'Then in time, to some other husband. The count married me only because he craves Normandy, and believes he will take the duchy at your vassalage to France. You have had reason before now to distrust Anjou, in the time of his father. That is the ambition both of them keep, and now that Fulk is king in Jerusalem it gives weight to whatever his son may decide. Geoffrey has decided already; he cares nothing for England. I care greatly. Women have ruled before; King Alfred's daughter ruled Mercia alone, and is remembered as a maker of peace.'

'England is more than Mercia, and times have altered since the Lady Ethelflaeda's day. What is it you would have me do for you?' He considered what she had said about Normandy; no doubt it was true, being the young brute's sole ambition. A son to inherit both realms would be the answer; what had they done about that? He asked her, forthrightly.

'We do not deal together,' she said coldly. 'I will not suffer him in my bed after the first. He goes to others.'

'Then he must come back to yours, or other arrangements will be made for the duchy after my death, of which you keep reminding me.'

'I pray that it will not happen for long. Take me back with you to England.'

'I have but lately left it, but you may return with me to Rouen while we investigate this matter.' He had, he knew, an arrangement already to meet the new pope, perhaps in a few months; Mathilde could put in an appearance then, and present herself. If the Angevin was excluded from such a meeting, it might make him mend his manners. Henry's anger rose; the prospect of Normandy's rule by any but his own blood was not to be considered. Yet this woman was the only means whereby it could be directly achieved. He needed time to think; he told her she might collect her gear, and travel back in his company.

They left Bec lonely amidst its trees, and the quiet which Herluin had coveted, and Anselm had inherited, came down again after the sound of hooves had died away.

The king left his daughter Mathilde at Rouen, where she was certainly happier than at Le Mans or Angers, and himself, in unusual turmoil of mind, rode off to hunt by the Seine. He invited Stephen's elder brother Count Theobald to join him, knowing well enough why he had done so without the empress's company. He was still undecided about the future, and wanted to assess Theobald's replies to certain questions: after all, as the elder brother he might resent the preference of the younger. Nevertheless Stephen's Boulogne marriage had added to his eligibility as England's heir, while Theobald himself had married yet another Matilda, daughter of a local count.

They hunted, then stretched their legs at the day's end before a fire which shut out the encroaching cold. Replete with venison and wine, the king spoke slowly.

'What do you think of Stephen? He seems to favour Cistercian thought, judging from his gifts to the order in the north of England. I cannot myself see that it becomes a ruler to be celibate, as they recommend.' The austere dwellers by clear waters, in chosen valleys in elected silence, would have all men virgin and dedicated to God. Theobald laughed, and picked a shred of meat from between his teeth. 'Stephen is no celibate,' he said. 'His marriage is fortunate, and but for the vow to your daughter the empress, might fit him to rule England better than any when the need arises. You have asked me for my opinion, and I give it. While England and Normandy are one, my uncle, France will be an enemy. Were there again two realms, separately ruled, it would be seen as less of a threat by Paris. I myself would guard Normandy for Stephen were he king of England.'

'It seemed to me that you might have ambitions to be king there yourself, as the elder.' He did not comment on what else the count had implied: he was gleaning opinions, no more. Theobald answered smoothly, as was his way.

'You know well, my respected uncle, none better, that he who has the crown set on his head is king. However to me England is a foreign island; I belong here, in Blois and Champagne. It is true that Clairvaux, Abbot Bernard's first foundation, began here; but I do not want to follow its course into England or any other place. Our mother chose to become a Cluniac at Marcigny, like Henry my brother elsewhere, also like the foundation at Lewes my aunt Gundreda, and her husband, began after visiting the mother house in Burgundy and experiencing great hospitality there. They had meant to go to Rome, as you know, but were prevented by the wars then between pope and emperor. They say Henry IV's son, the late emperor, is not dead after all.' Count Theobald had drunk too much wine; it was the wrong thing to say to the empress's father, let alone the reminder about de Warenne's mother, his sister.

'They say many things,' remarked King Henry coldly.

Count Theobald rode in company with the king to Chartres to meet the pope. By then it was Epiphany, and very cold, with thin flakes of snow falling, to presage more later on. Through the drifting veil they could see the dark caverns and grottoes which had survived the many burnings and invasions of this famous place where the tunic of the Annunciation was kept, having been given to Chartres by Charlemagne's grandson in his time. Henry remembered hearing how it had survived, in its reliquary, the fire which had swept through the upper part of the church, having been placed by chance in a vault. He heard his nephew recount again the miracle of how their old ancestor Rollo had been induced by its means to embrace Christianity.

'He had intended to sack the place, as the Danes and the men of Aquitaine had done before him. However when the bishop held up the sacred tunic like a banner, Rollo and his Vikings turned and fled, and shortly after that had themselves baptised and made peace with France.'

That last might be possible again today; besides the pope, there waited emissaries from the French king. The man responsible was present modestly, eyes lowered and wearing his white Cistercian habit; Abbot Bernard of Clairvaux himself, by reason of whose known prejudices Henry had not brought his daughter the empress with him. It was enough for the good abbot to have to survey a former lecher such as himself. The eyes raised themselves once to his own, and were like liquid fire: the abbot himself was worn to a bone with mortifications, and looked older than his thirty-eight years.

The pope, on the other hand, was bland, and it was of interest to remember that he was that same former Cardinal Guidoni who had given the general absolution to the kneeling pilgrims about to set out for the first advance on the Holy Sepulchre, almost a generation ago. That had been after the inspired sermon of the late Pope Urban II, in France; but Normandy had responded in the person of Curthose and in the elder Stephen of Blois, father of Theobald and young Stephen and Henry. Innocent II greeted king and count now, recalling that Countess Adela had herself been the mediator, in person, in part of the early dispute with Rome and Anselm. He enquired in courteous Latin how the countess did.

'She is at peace in her convent in Marcigny, and will see no one,' Adela's son said. His mother prayed there for the soul of his father; no doubt she had not forgiven herself for sending her husband back again to die after he had turned back, homesick, at Antioch. The world seemed a small place; they debated various matters, while the snow fell ever more thickly outside the windows. Money was to be given to Fontevrault, the new foundation where young Matilda the Audelin's bride had immured herself by now, under its first abbess Petronilla. Henry hid his lack of sympathy with this fashion for removing oneself forever from the world; the world had to go on, and it was men like himself who ensured that that would happen. He watched the young prince Louis, sent to receive the pope's blessing, come forward and kneel devoutly, his long hair falling about him like that of the ancient Mérovings. Everyone parted friends, with a promise by the pope that he would visit Rouen shortly, and then would meet the empress.

The empress wore her jewelled crown for the pope's visit to Rouen, which gratified her father. It was fitting that his daughter should shine as brightly as any in this assembly of distinction, perhaps the apogee of his double reign. Here in old Rollo's capital were gathered famous persons; again, the austere white-clad figure of the abbot of Clairvaux, somehow outvying with his fierce, silent presence the splendour of the prelates' robes; a fussy little abbot of low origins named Suger of St Denis, who had achieved power in France and was said to be able to heal divisions anywhere; the bishops of Chartres and of Rouen; and, also with an outlandish name, Bozon from Angers, making provision in the absence of his lord that Normandy was to be desired, the marriage itself not forgotten. However Count Geoffrey had not been invited, nor had the brothers of Blois. Henry had noted with irony that in any absence of Mathilde, either Stephen or Theobald were assiduous in their presence at court and council; but today, when she was the centre of all eyes, they had not asked to come. She progressed into the cathedral, handsome, crowned and dignified, a worthy successor of the Conqueror's line. *And when the iron brood in the land shall fail.* He must remember that part of the prophecy, and guard as might be done against it; it could not be avoided, in the nature of things, that the white dragon's blood should intrude. Nevertheless Mathilde herself was nearing thirty, and if she was to bear sons they would be children still when he, the king, should die. He had not been well lately, with discomfort in his innards when he rode. He set that thought aside and watched the procession from where he sat, himself robed and crowned, beside the pope. De Warenne, as assiduous as any now that he was failing with old age, had lost teeth and had an heir, was present; so was good Robert of Gloucester, Henry's own beloved son. It was a further irony that he of all men was forever beyond reach of the crown, and too loyal to try to grasp it.

A grant was made at the council to the abbey of Cluny, which should please de Warenne as his parents had founded the daughter priory at Lewes; otherwise, there was some matter relating to a gift to the church by one Robert de Brus, who had lands in Yorkshire and was already known to the king. Henry remembered de Brus without knowing why; he was not present today.

Later, in a day or two, there were gifts made to Bec, where Waleran de Meulan was a patron. The empress surprised her father by saying that she wanted to be buried there.

'It is not notable enough for you,' he told her severely. Mathilde replied that did not matter; she often went there, the place brought her peace. 'That was why I asked you to come to me there, my father,' she said. Henry did not answer; he was unaware of any affection for her, she was a pawn, no more. In all of his life he knew he had only loved certain people; his mother, his first son Robert, also, for some reason, William the old prior of Bec, with whom Henry had himself sat as he lay dying; and the lost Audelin. There had been certain feeling aroused by some; fear and admiration by his father; resentment, even hatred, by his brothers; toleration for the formidable Adela, who was the only one of his sisters he had had the chance to know. The one of her sons to have inherited most of her strength was, he decided, Henry, late of Winchester; that long-headed young churchman would always advance his family.

Abbot Bernard had made himself listen with distaste as the empress took it upon herself to speak to him before he left to return to his quiet valley. A woman at all was unwelcome, one who had left her husband doubly so; his own task had been to bring the pope into accord with King Henry, as matters in England were taking too independent a turn; but this woman might, after all, rule there.

'When I was in Germany we talked a great deal about the teaching of Peter Abélard,' she said. 'It is tragic that the brilliance of such a mind should be lost.' An outrage had been performed on

Abélard which made it impossible for him to obtain church preferment: he had been drugged and castrated. Before that, he was said to have married his mistress, Héloïse, like him a scholar. They had a son. The story seemed pitiful to Mathilde, who occasionally took an interest in others besides herself.

'He is atoning for his misdeeds by manual labour at Cluny,' snapped the abbot of Clairvaux. Abélard's affair with a young woman concerned him less than the former theologian's views on the Trinity, which were not those officially approved.

Matihilde continued to press her point; she was not intimidated by this monk who evidently thought the world should stop breeding. 'St Paul assumed that all of us were about to be taken up into the clouds and therefore should not marry, but that was long ago,' she continued. 'The world has existed even since the year 1,000, when everybody waited in fear and trembling for it to end.'

'Our Lord said no warning would be given,' replied Bernard of Clairvaux. 'Look to your own marriage,' and turned away. She had not asked him concerning further matters which troubled her; he was not in sympathy, it was evident.

The pope rose finally, and proceeded outside to give the waiting crowds his blessing, warmed by the pale May sunshine. By August, the empress was thinking, she and her father would have left here and returned to England, perhaps by the feast of St Peter ad Vincula; and perhaps, once there, the chains could be struck from her wretched marriage, as had happened by a miracle to the apostle chained long ago in his prison. The gates had opened, and St Peter had walked out free.

Mathilde spent a glad month in England. Not only was it the first time she had her father's company in a respite from great affairs, but she was able, in the peace of his law, to ride freely about the land alone or with a small following; often in the company of

Brien FitzCount and her own half-brother Robert of Gloucester. She could talk freely with these men as equals, in the way she had been used to talk with her German advisers, though these were less obsequious and less formal; but the empress had ceased to demand as much formality now.

The land which she hoped would be her own was her delight; green England, with its royal forests where she could hunt, its fields where a hawk could fly, its markets and fairs and squat wooden Saxon churches. Germany had been a predictable land, England was forever unpredictable, which no doubt was why her father had coveted it, and so did she. There was an independence in the glances of the English which challenged her Norman blood; she would rule them with understanding, but firmness. Lacking a strong ruler they would fall again into factions, little kingdoms such as there had once been: Kent and Wessex and Mercia and Bernicia and Deira, then the north. Her uncle David ruled there now in peace likewise; he would be her ally. He was to be her host, hers and her father's, soon at a great meeting at Northampton, again to elicit fealty to her as Lady of England and, it was hoped, to declare her Angevin marriage formally at an end. She had said little of that to her father since Bec.

The court of pleas at Northampton was set to take place on the birthday of Our Lady, the eighth day of September. Before that, an urgent message had come unexpectedly for the empress. There was no time to do more than send word to the king, who was at Waltham. At once, Mathilde set out, taking little gear with her and only a few servitors. There had been a good Roman road between Deva and Londinium. It still served for swift travel.

The king made his own way to the old Danish meeting-place of Northampton, once the heart of the former Danelaw; its burr could still be heard in the speech of the inhabitants, many of whom had fair hair almost white. King David rode out to greet him, and the two monarchs feasted at the high table together. David of Scotland spoke with pride of his son.

'I named him Henry after you, and he looks to take you as his model in wisdom. He is learned, pious – he could be a monk, but must not – and, God be thanked, has stronger health than his sisters.' Next day the king was taken to see little Henry of Huntingdon riding at the tilt, watched by the two pale princesses who were his senior by a few years only. But for him, the same problem would confront Scotland as troubled them now in England; the prospect of a woman's rule.

The king sent for the child Henry later on, and gave him his blessing while secretly resenting his handsome strength: why could his own lost Audelin not have lived? As for the empress, if she did not return he would open the court of pleas without her. He had already ensured what the vote as to her marriage would be. For the look of the thing, however, they should renew their fealty for England and Normandy: Geoffrey of Anjou must not be encouraged to think that his union, in any case, counted for nothing. More than ever Henry, increasingly ill in body, knew himself a watcher rather than a partaker in events. Theobald or Geoffrey could handle Normandy, Stephen or Mathilde England; alliance between the two sets of rulers would ensure that France did not continue to regard with a wary eye one realm instead of two, though in secret the two would remain one. Until the blood of the white dragon prevailed, it was the best he himself could contrive.

The empress returned, and as before asked to see him privately. She was travel-stained, but her face was cold and inscrutable.

'What has happened?' he asked her with equal coldness. 'It seemed that you might keep the assembly waiting; many have come far.'

'The assembly matters nothing. My marriage to Anjou is no

marriage. My first husband the emperor was alive till two days since. I was with him when he died, having sent for me.'

'This is madness,' he told her. 'Where did all this happen?' She could not, in the time, he was thinking, have been overseas.

He heard as much as she knew, which was enough to determine him as to his own action. A dying man had been brought by river up the Dee estuary, intending no doubt to travel nearer the court.

'I would not have known him,' Mathilde said. 'He was nothing but a skeleton with living eyes, and his hair and beard had turned white. He had wanted greatly to say farewell to me. He sent a messenger with the one word "Tildchen", which is what he used to call me, and where to come. I set out, and when I was brought to him it was at the monastery which lies to the west of Chester. He died within an hour of my arriving, but he knew I had come to him. He died with my hand in his. He was always good to me.' Her eyes held tears.

'This cannot have happened,' he said. 'You have been the victim of a deception. Henry V died almost seven years ago. You have married again. Do you want all Europe to laugh at you as the count of Anjou's whore?'

She was trembling. 'What I have told you is the truth,' she said. 'I know it was my husband. He had parted with all worldly things, as he intended; but before he died sent for me.' She knew he had come to her there, at the west of Chester; he would know of the court arranged to meet at Northampton, all men did.

'If you continue to believe this crazed thing, you are not fit to govern England. I will appoint your cousin Stephen of Blois and Mortain, my sister's son, instead as my successor. He is liked by the people, especially the Londoners, because of his wife and the trade she brings. I will direct this court of pleas to give you no credence. You may please yourself in the matter, one way or the other.' He avoided looking at her face; when she had heard the mention of Stephen she had drawn a hissing breath.

'You devil,' she said then. 'I am nothing to you but a brood-mare. You would cast me aside as though I were not of your blood, not your daughter, your only true heir. You -' Like Juliana, she would have raised her nails to his eyes; he struck her aside.

'Leave our presence,' he said formally. 'You may enter the great hall as you will, or not; the decision is one for my lords in council, not for yourself.'

He went out, and left her staring after him. He had already dismissed in his mind the tale of the returned emperor. It would be possible, if necessary, to render an exhumed body unidentifiable; but there existed other means, less troublesome, to hand.

The empress had been received by the queen of Scots in Maud's own elegant apartment in the new palace of Northampton. Robert of Gloucester joined the two kings, with only Henry among them wearing his crown, and went down into the hall. Maud herself turned back after greeting the assembly as hostess: she was not wont to attend great matters, being more at home with her daily tasks and her children. The bishops and nobles stood while the great of the land seated themselves at the high dais; then the council was opened, with a prayer to God that it might be guided aright. The prayer itself was made by Thurstan of York, the contentious bishop of the earlier dispute with Canterbury. Everyone sat then, and matters in hand commenced. King Henry made his speech remaining seated; he was in discomfort by now when standing or walking. Everyone had remarked on the grey colour of his face. His son Gloucester sat close by, at the foot of the dais: he seldom left his father for long these days.

'We are here assembled to decide on the fate of the kingdom at my death. That will take place when God wills. For a successor to be appointed is desirable. You have already sworn fealty to my daughter, who is here present. Are you prepared to renew it?'

A rough noble named Hugh Bigod spoke up. 'We swore fealty on the understanding that no marriage would be arranged for your daughter without our consent. It was so arranged, and has produced no heirs. The fealty therefore is no longer valid. I speak as I feel. Others may do likewise.'

A babble broke out; the sight of the empress seated above them, handsome and regal, silenced many. 'She ruled well in Germany,' shouted one. 'What is that to do with us?' they replied. 'She is thirty years old, and has no children.'

'Whom will you have to rule you if not the king's daughter? I will aid my sister in all things.' It was Robert of Gloucester, speaking clearly from his place. His presence and his words convinced many; then someone recalled that that was all very well for England, but Normandy was to be ruled as well; and the empress had a husband; why did she not return to him? The county of Anjou would govern Normandy on her behalf, the earl of Gloucester, England.

'You are making me of no account,' said Mathilde in a low voice. 'You cannot be in two places, Lady,' replied Ranulf of Chester, who was present; had he known, he could have witnessed the recent death of the emperor in his own county. 'My father contrives it,' replied Henry's daughter. The king himself sat silent, knowing already which way the vote would go.

Thurstan of York stood up, and faced King David of Scotland, who had risen likewise in support of his niece. Seven years later, bishop and king were to meet on opposite sides in battle; but for the time, words were smooth.

'We will renew our fealty to the countess of Anjou if she will return to her husband, and make heirs for England. Otherwise, nothing is certain for any of us.'

There was uproar, and the king rose at last and silenced it with his hand. For the last time, the famous roar of the Lion of Justice sounded in the hall.

'Display your fealty by raising your right hands,' he commanded. 'Those who do not will be counted.'

A forest of hands raised themselves, including the bishop of Salisbury's, whose homage in the event was to prove questionable. Most were still calling out that the empress must return to her husband. Having witnessed the homage, Mathilde rose. She turned to her uncle and host.

'I will leave them to their manly deliberations,' she said. 'Take me back to your wife.'

King David led her from the hall, the object of many curious and avid glances; what ailed the count of Anjou that he did not crave so fine a woman in his bed? After they had gone out it was stated by the king that the count in fact wanted his wife to return, not having overlooked the promise of Normandy. De Warenne spoke up, as if unwilling to be left out of proceedings even now.

'They say he has prepared a fitting welcome for such a virago,' he mumbled, lacking teeth as ever. The coarse laughter that followed was heard by the empress as she left the hall, escorted on one side by David of Scotland and on the other by Robert of Gloucester, who had risen also and gone out with her. At the door of the queen's apartments she turned, white-faced.

'Tell them, when you go back as you must,' she said, 'that I will return to Anjou, and that their homage is remembered.'

They kissed her hands, and left her.

Kind Queen Maud was waiting, and did her utmost to comfort the stony-faced woman. 'Take heart,' she said. 'My own first marriage was not happy, and for long I wept; but the children came, my two sons Simon and Waldef, and were a solace to me. You will find the same. Come now and see Harry. He has solaced all our grief.'

Prince Henry of Scotland was again at the tilt, riding at the ring with determination. The September sun shone on his fair hair, the hair of his lost grandfather Waltheof, last earl of Northumbria, son of Siward of old fame. Waltheof's daughter, King David's queen, regarded her last-born son with pride.

'He bears the blood of many kings,' she said. 'I pray that he may father more.' Had she known, Henry of Huntingdon's bride was to be Earl Warren's young daughter, and from them both would spring a heroic line, the Conqueror's blood mingling with that of the ancient kings of Scots and the old royal line of England. All that was in the future; Prince Henry now was a carefree boy, doing what he liked next best to learning under his tutors and saying his prayers. They turned away, Mathilde a little comforted; if she could bear such a son, it would be worth enduring what she knew awaited her.

Next day, she rode south, having bidden farewell to her father. She was to see him again.

3

WILLIAM DE ALBINI, the strongest knight in England, was riding alone by his own winding river, his great Norway hawk on his powerful wrist. From time to time he let her fly upwards, taking such pleasure as he might at the sight of her strong beating wings and her skill in bringing down the bloodstained prey after pursuit in the sky. It occurred to him, not for the first time, to wonder why the sight of blood was necessary for pleasure; but he himself had little other, having loved the same woman now for twelve years, from first sight, and still the king did not die.

It was disloyal, no doubt, to hope that this would soon happen; and of all things Albini was loyal, as much so as Robert of Gloucester himself. He had served King Henry at war and in council, though he did not frequent the court lest his love be perceived and gossip hurt the queen. He was not an easy dissembler and knew he could not hide it. She knew of it, he was certain; although word of it had never been spoken between them. He remained merely Adeliza's faithful knight, her devoted servitor. Not long ago he had been host to the king and queen, here at Arundel; and had had to endure the thought of his love in the old man's bed. It was not, however, probable by now that Henry, in his state of health, was a husband to her. They blamed her for barrenness; he, William de Albini, could give her children; he was convinced of that, but either way it mattered nothing. He dared not imagine the delight of lying with his dear love in his arms, wrapped close in bed, warmed from the cold, kissed into gladness; her rose-leaf prettiness was fading, her eyes anxious, always on the old sick husband's behalf; he himself would not have her otherwise than as she was, devoted and careful; but it was hard to wait, while the years passed, and to ride home, as he would do now, with the cooling prey in his saddle-bag and no welcome waiting except that of his favourite dogs.

He could have married elsewhere, he knew; could have kept a mistress, but did not fancy it. He would wait, if necessary all his life, for his lady; and he dared not pray that the king's death would come soon.

The Norway hawk had flown back to her master's wrist. Albini smoothed her feathers, fed her a gobbet of meat in reward, and rode home. A line of some minstrelsy he had lately heard sung came to him. *His hawk, and his hound, and his lady fair*. He had, after all, the first two. The third might perhaps soon, after all, be his. He must continue to have patience, and hope. He knew Adeliza was troubled about her stepdaughter the empress, of whom she was fond. The count of Anjou was rumoured to have thrashed his wife on her return. That was distasteful, given the young man's hopes for Normandy. Few men knew love, evidently; he himself would regard every part of Adeliza's body as precious, to be cherished and respected. There was however a saying that to beat a woman was to make her more readily pregnant. So far, there had been no rumour of that out of Anjou: and it was more than a year since the empress's return there.

The king could no longer ride to see his lions at Woodstock, and had himself borne into the park one day by litter. He told the bearers to leave him, and remained for as long as he might, staring into the great beasts' golden eyes. It was said that if one gave a lion look for look, there was no danger; and there were many legends of men who had lions as friends. He himself wondered, not for the first time, if he was closer to animals than to man. Man he observed drily; the lions he watched with respect. He remembered the camel, long dead by now, that his brother-in-law had sent him from Scotland. It had shown only contempt for him, which had amused him; God made varied creatures, and none were hypocrites. God had however seen fit to save man, and not the animals, who were without sin. Had he himself sinned beyond forgiveness? One of his most trusted servants, Roger of Salisbury, he had promoted to a bishopric and to power because of his speed in dispatching a mass. There was probably no place in heaven for either of them; what else was waiting after death, the worm that never died, the flame that consumed forever? He had however made gifts to abbeys and churches; perhaps that would save him. Good Mald prayed for his soul, no doubt, where she was now; and good Adeliza would do the same. He had been fortunate in his wives. He had attained all his father had promised. 'Only wait, and all will be yours.' All was his now, and he took no pleasure in it.

The well-fed lions yawned, showing yellowed teeth. They were accustomed to the sight of the sick old man in the litter.

Robert of Gloucester was fond of his father the king, with a cool understanding nobody else dared feel. They were near enough of an age to be companions; it had begun in Robert's boyhood, when the exiled young prince who was his father had taken him away from Caen, where his mother was, and had travelled about with him on the borders of France and Germany, forever restless, forever planning the next move in the game of royal chess. Robert had become faithful, trustworthy and loyal because the king was all he had; now, with power, an earldom and a rich marriage, he maintained these qualities and would use them on behalf of his sister when it was time.

The marriage made for him some years before had been with FitzHamon's daughter, whose father had been one of the New Forest hunting-party long ago and had adhered to the king then and since. His daughter Mabel, who had at first complained that her bridegroom was nameless and landless, had settled down to make an excellent wife who bore handsome children. The fact that they bore the name of Fitzroy by now was less of a favour than it might have been, as the name was also shared by the son of Welsh Nest. Nevertheless, the earl of Gloucester knew that he was a fortunate man in his marriage, and could gladly enough have stayed at home in idleness, without responsibility or danger. However it was increasingly evident that the king was ill.

By Christmas, at Windsor, Henry had taken to his bed. Gloucester waited by it now. His father's face was grey, as always of late years: he was in a bout of depression, some of the reasons for which he gave to his son. Earl Warren, for long now his assiduous follower, wanted to betroth his heir, the third William, to the young daughter of William Talvas, who had de Bellême blood. Such a marriage would help to strengthen any claim the earl might make in alliance with France; it was probable that his early ambitions merely slumbered and had not died. Moreover, any news Henry had from Anjou indicated that the empress and her husband continued to disagree, like fighting dogs.

Robert was smiling, however. 'You bear good news, I hope,' said the king. He had felt tired and old; did it matter so greatly who ruled England when he was dead? He sent gifts, at Christmas and Easter, through Gloucester to his blinded brother, and had always seen to it that Curthose lacked nothing in the way of food and drink. Had tidings come from Cardiff? Failing himself, Curthose was no doubt the next heir; but a blind king could not reign.

Moreover, young Louis of France having married his Aquitanian heiress, and said to be greatly enamoured of her, there might well be a continuing block of adversity in sons of that marriage, lording it over lands that stretched from Paris to Toulouse. No man could live forever to ward off disaster from sons and grandsons and nephews: some other must take charge.

Gloucester's smile had broadened. 'The best possible news, my father,' he said. 'The empress is with child. She did not send word to you till the thing was certain. He – we must pray for a son – should be born, all going well, in March. Pray for an easy labour for my sister. She is not young to bear for the first time.'

He did not add what everyone by now knew, that the begetting of the child had been contrived without pleasure. Henry's colour improved; he almost smiled, and sent permission for the de Warenne marriage at once. God help the third earl, thought Gloucester, who knew the sturdy good-natured boy; his bride, another Adela, was a spitfire, a true Bellême. The king, had he known, was beyond caring; he grudged nothing to anyone now, even Gundreda's descent. It was his grandson, not hers, who would inherit.

He did not however cross seas instantly to see the grandson. For one thing his health would not yet allow, although it had improved at once with the news. For another, he did not desire to behold a puling infant, who might die as many did. He would wait for the colour of the boy's eyes to emerge, knowing that a baby's at the first were always blue; and would wait to obtain some estimate of character once the child had an appearance to show. The first hair must fall out, the baldness come; then a christened being became a soul. Thirdly, there were matters claiming his attention on this side of the water, such as the rights of London barons and citizens to be buried where they chose and to have their own priest follow the coffin. He himself knew that he wanted to be buried at Reading, the abbey he had built, where the hand of St James now rested that the empress had brought to him from Spain.

It was Lammas before he set out, and the weather had turned wild, so much so that roofs were blown off houses. The king lay on board ship in total darkness; there was an eclipse of the sun. He pondered other such heard-of things, wondering what this portended; there had been a great hairy comet seen in the sky before Hastings, another earlier, at the Scots' taking of Lothian in Cnut's reign. There was no need to feel now, as some did, that the end of the world had come; but the king was glad when the sun again shed its light. He would lie buried long enough, in the dark, as now, alone.

The ship crossed the Channel safely, storms or none. As Rufus had said long ago, no king had ever drowned. Henry remembered that he had not been able to look his last on England; it had been dark then, in the midst of the eclipse.

At length, he had the curious experience of looking down into his own grey eyes. They were not even innocent, and were hard as pebbles. His grandson, Henry Plantagenet, however, had red hair.

Henry Plantagenet was not a handsome child. There was strength; he looked already, at six months, as if he could lift a fair weight in each hand. The hands themselves were large, ungainly and without pretension as to noble birth. In fact, the empress's son, with a crop of red stubble sprouting anew on his bullet head, resembled nobody more than the Conqueror's maternal forebears, the working tanners of Falaise. He had a belligerent expression that would have done credit to Robert de Bellême himself. He thumped at a piece of coral which had been given him on which to bite, as if he preferred to use it as a hammer and would grow his own teeth unaided. He was square in body, without the lithe grace of his father or the handsome dignity of his mother. His private parts were enormous, as a baby's often are: but somehow it was evident that they would keep pace. It was easy to imagine his legs bowed already, though he had not yet been in the saddle; like the count his father he would, no doubt, never walk when he could ride.

The king surveyed him, aware of one thing; this was the lion's whelp, who would one day reign. The prophecy had been clear; the eaglet would try and fail, and the Sagittary, the centaur, Stephen, would be overcome by peaceful means in the end. Then the second Henry would reign; and it would be a strong reign, like his own. If he were to die now, he would not have lived in vain. He felt, nevertheless, slightly better than of late. He could even think of the other grandson briefly seen and left behind in England. Young Richard de Clare, son of his own daughter by Bess Beaumont, was three years old now and could already pull a bowstring. His father Pembroke jested and called him Strongbow. No doubt he and the lion's whelp would meet, but not yet. Much would happen between.

The king embraced his daughter, who was already pregnant again, and sick accordingly; this second child would be troublesome in her, it was too soon, hardly more than a year allowed to elapse between the births. Henry instructed her to come to Rouen at the due time, Pentecost. He rode back then, pleased with his visit. The count had made himself scarce, but was evidently proud of his son. Henry returned with a sense of achievement, seeing the Devil's Tower rise with predictable affection; that child he had left behind in Le Mans had the devil's blood in him as well as all the rest. What hands! They, and his parts, would seduce women. It was a pity he, the elder Henry, would almost certainly be dead.

*

At the beginning of Lent, the king received word that Curthose was so. His brother had been over eighty years of age, and had been a prisoner for twenty-eight years.

When he had leisure, the king heard more of it, chiefly from Robert of Gloucester, who had seen the old duke as he was dying. 'He would not eat,' said Robert. 'The gift of a scarlet gown you sent him at Christmas had a tear in it, and he cried bitterly, saying his royal brother sent him cast-off ragged clothing and he might as well die.' It was a curious and pathetic saying from one who had once had his clothes stolen regularly from him by his servants because he slept late, long ago in Normandy.

The king remembered that it was his own ruthless daughter who had persuaded him to ward Robert Curthose with Gloucester, for safety, rather than with Roger of Salisbury. It would have come to the same thing, doubtless; but he had obliged her. He refused to do so again now, over the matter of receiving William Talvas, de Bellême's son, whom the empress regarded as her supporter; but Henry would never trust one of that blood. The man's daughter was married now to de Warenne's son; one had heard that they sparred constantly, like the empress here and her husband. Despite young Henry's birth, and the new pregnancy, the sound of their raucous quarrelling came almost audibly to Rouen. He began to be weary of them, and to think again of Stephen meantime; only meantime, till the lion's whelp was grown.

He returned again to memories of Curthose. Changes from one gaol to another, Devizes, Bristol, Cardiff; these had made up the sum of life for the man who had once fought at Ascalon, capturing, to give to the Sepulchre, the emir's standard of silver and gold; whom no man could unseat from the saddle; whose taper the

Holy Spirit had lighted three times in the church at Jerusalem, inviting him to be king. Had God punished Robert for refusal? Fulk of Anjou, Count Geoffrey's father, reigned there now; there was a son of that second marriage.

Gloucester his own son told Henry a strange thing, one of the many he had heard from his prisoner in Cardiff over the years. One day during the siege of the Holy City a brown-skinned man in Arab dress had come to Robert Curthose, desiring speech. 'He spoke French,' said Gloucester, 'and offered his services. He said who he was, or rather who he had been; and that is the reason, my father, that you only hear the tale now.' The man had been one of the murderers, long ago in Normandy, of old Mabel of Montgomery, mother to Robert de Bellême. The brothers, three of them who owed her much wrong, had watched her bathing in the river, then as Henry already knew had followed her back into the castle. 'They set upon her and cut off her head, seizing it by the hair and taking it with them,' said Gloucester. He went on with the tale he had heard from Curthose. 'They had hidden themselves from the king's wrath – it had been the Conqueror then – in Apulia for a time, then Sicily, then with the emperor Alexius in Constantinople. Nevertheless the de Bellême family, and the king-duke himself, had continued to search for the murderers of Mabel, much as she had deserved her fate. "In the end I changed my dress, my religion and my name, forsaking Christ for Islam. I have lived as an infidel Turk for twenty years. Now I would serve you, Duke Robert of Normandy, because you are a famous leader and my overlord, and I would atone for my sin." '

'He said all that to me,' relayed Gloucester. The man's name had been Hugh Baduel, one of the de Giroye clan old Mabel had persecuted, often by her accustomed means of poison. Hugh's knowledge of the language, customs and probable movements of the enemy had proved useful to the Christian army. His father had been a Norman knight; whether or not he had returned with Curthose Gloucester did not know. There had followed wealth, power and fame, the marriage with lovely Sybil of Conversano, the conceiving of the Clito on the high rock of Mont St Michel, the archangel's place above the sound of the everlasting sea.

'The only sea he saw, by the end, was the Severn,' Gloucester remembered. 'The last thing he ever watched was an oak tree there, split by lightning or a sword, on the shore opposite his high window; there was once a Roman camp across there on a slight rise. After he was blinded he began to learn Welsh for his diversion, and I ordered them to let the speakers in to him, as he could no longer do harm. They made him a bard in the end, a high honour among them. He wrote a poem in Welsh about the remembered oak.'

'What did it say?' asked the king. He reminded himself that he had often sent little luxuries to Curthose: he had nothing with which to reproach himself. He could have done no other than blind his brother, by the end. There would have been more trouble otherwise.

'I can remember one line only. *Woe! To him who has looked on what is not death*. It has rhythm in Welsh, but I do not know the tongue.'

'Well, he is dead now,' said the king. He ordered a handsome tomb, with an effigy; one leg was to be crossed over the other, to indicate the great pilgrimage. Curthose now had journeyed on a longer one still. He himself would soon join both his brothers, Rufus no doubt duly emerging from the further shades.

Nevertheless Henry had felt better in health since first sight of the lion's whelp; his own life had been renewed in that other. He even contrived to hunt again, downing the discomfort he felt in the saddle and refusing nostrums from his physician, Grimbauld. A good gallop would rid it; if one gave way to pain and old age, it conquered. There was bad news lately from Wales, of unrest there; he must soon return, although Mathilde and her husband the count were still squabbling, not unproductively; the young cockerel seemed to tread her at will, she was a third time pregnant after giving birth safely to a second son last year in Rouen. At her age, it was a matter for encouragement.

It was the twenty-fifth of November, 1135, when Henry rode out to hunt at Lyons-la-Forêt. It was the anniversary of the Audelin's drowning fifteen years ago, and in other years he had mourned for all of that day. Now, there was hope; seen in the swelling buds for next year, already manifest among the red-brown clinging of last, in the branches of the great beech trees, older than Rollo's time; the silver trunks reared, with birdsong and scampering red squirrels in the branches, and the sound of the oncoming hooves of their horses was soft on last season's trodden leaves. The king raised his head and sniffed the fresh morning air. He felt life coursing through his veins again. This forest, where the old dukes had loved to hunt, was like his father's New Forest across the water, the place where his own reign had begun. He was the same man now as he had been then; life had taught him little he had not already known. If it was all to do again, he would act no differently; except that he would hold back a certain ship at Barfleur till her captain was sober. Young flesh, turned soon to the shape of fishes. He must not think of that today, riding on.

They brought down a stag, and later rode home with it, gutted and tied to poles by the feet. The king looked forward to his dinner; he was hungry, and they set before him first of all a dish of glistening fried eels, caught fresh from the Seine. Grimbauld shook his head. 'Do not eat them,' he said with the familiarity of long acquaintance. 'They are not good for you, my lord king.'

The king laughed, and shovelled the fish in his mouth. It was a good way to end the day, his favourite dish served in a subtle sauce.

Tomorrow they would hunt again. He loved the forests. Merlin of the prophecies was entombed not far off in one, Brocéliande.

Before the meal was ended, he had a seizure. They saw him fall sideways, his mouth spilling out half-chewed food. They carried him to bed and sent for a priest. The archbishop of Rouen came, having received word in time. He had already ordered prayers to be said for the king-duke in all Norman churches. It was not yet time to toll the bells; perhaps the king-duke would recover.

Henry was aware of churning dark, and a sound inside his head of angry bees. Where was Adeliza? She ought to be here to bathe his temples. He could make out nothing clearly, except the shape of other figures standing by his bed. He knew his son Gloucester was there, holding both his hands; good Gloucester, steadfast to the end. That it was the end Henry already knew; and watched himself as if from somewhere else. The place he found himself in was doubtful; two men stood waiting, one old and blind in a scarlet tunic, the other with saffron hair. At the same time he heard his own voice, mumbling a last confession. It would not, he supposed, be possible to make sense of the words. The archbishop gave absolution, and put the Host on his tongue: he only felt half of it, the other half being numb. Robert of Gloucester had held his hands till the last moment, when he had had by tradition to withdraw. He had felt his father's pulse bound strongly for a time, then fail. Shortly he came back to close the dead eyes. They should not, he was thinking, plunder the king's body after death as they had plundered the Conqueror's, leaving it tumbled naked on the floor. He himself would see all things arranged in seemly fashion, sending his father's body across seas to Reading, where the king had long desired to be buried.

Nine years later, after much war of his making, Geoffrey of Anjou was crowned duke of Normandy in the cathedral at Rouen. Once again, as at his earlier knightly vigil, he surveyed the Norman tombs. His father-on-law's was not among them; Geoffrey grinned inwardly. The king's corpse had stank so greatly that they had sewn it in a bull's hide for transport to England; it was said the surgeon who opened the Lion of Justice's brain to examine it had died of the stench.

Here, there still lay only old Rollo and his son Longsword; and Rollo had after all deepened the river here to take shipping, drained the marshes, anchored the islands, made his capital city firm on its base.

The same foresight, no doubt, had been handed down to old Henry, and from him to young Henry, one's own eldest son; a diamond in process of polishing, much trouble was being taken with his education; two years ago, at the age of nine, he had visited England and had returned safely despite Stephen's usurpation. It was doubtful however that the boy would, unlike his namesake, earn the name of Beauclerc after death for having left documents in so fair a hand. That had been because the old lecher was originally intended for the church.

His daughter, arrogant bitch that she still was, had borne oneself three sons, losing her health finally over the last, William, who was a milksop. The second, named Geoffrey, was a pest. Only Henry of them all was worth anything. He himself, their father, would continue the tradition of the ancient counts of Anjou, perhaps expand their empire still further in some manner; it remained to be seen.

Meantime, he, Geoffrey Plantagenet, had taken no part in his wife's recent antics in England, trying to redeem her inheritance there after Stephen of Blois had hastened over, on the advice of his churchman brother, and got himself crowned, Mathilde at the time being pregnant and unable to travel. A crown made a king; there had been civil war, and Mathilde herself had been chased at last out of London, riding astride in her ugly German fashion, and later had had to escape in a nightgown somewhere in the snow.

He had taken nothing to do with all of that, leaving Robert of Gloucester, who at first had sworn fealty to Stephen with the rest, and Brien FitzCount to aid her. He, Geoffrey, had strengthened the hold on Normandy for the sake of himself and his son. By now he had justified the hopes of all his ancestors, including the devil. Old King Henry, no doubt, was turning in his grave at Reading, still wrapped in the bull's hide.

Duke Geoffrey rose, crowned and handsome at thirty-five, and progressed out of the cathedral. He had seven years left to live.

The dowager queen – King Stephen's own queen, Matilda of Boulogne, showed great courage in the resulting civil war of the two claimants – had remained a widow for more than the prescribed year, in fact for two. Despite the pleadings of William de Albini that he had loved her long and faithfully, Adeliza hesitated to marry again; the church frowned on it. She prayed meticulously for the welfare of the late king's soul, and as promised had paid for two candles, one at Henry's head, the other at his feet, to burn in perpetuity in the abbey of Reading. Eventually she had pity on Albini, and allowed him to marry her, still fearful of sin. All should thereafter have been joy; but on the wedding night, discovering in course of his tender approaches that his bride still possessed a maidenhead at thirty-six, Albini let out an untoward oath which did not advance his cause.

'God's bones, madam, you mean to tell me that the old devil never—?'

She was disapproving; he had spoken ill of the dead. Aware as she undoubtedly became of the pleasures of being cherished, of the gradual filling of the nursery at Arundel with thriving and beautiful children, the erstwhile Fair Maid of Brabant felt herself increasingly to blame for the worsening state of things in England; she should have given the late king sons like these, then all this trouble up and down the land – one heard really dreadful things, especially when the empress visited Arundel in mid-campaign – would never have had to occur. Adeliza's mind could not encompass the fact that any lack of replacements for the vanished Audelin had been by no means her fault; it had been assumed that she was barren, and now she had ceased to be so and, furthermore, knew a contented happiness she could not deny. The whole thing made her, in fact, feel guilty; and the more de Albini's tenderness and devotion increased, the guiltier Adeliza felt. It was as though the dead king's iron will reached out to her from the grave. She had not done her duty at the time, and it was sinful to do it now, let alone to enjoy it.

In the end, no doubt taking with her the reproachful shade of the Lion of Justice himself, she entered a convent, leaving behind tearful children and a grief-stricken husband, and stayed there for the remainder of her days. By that time, few in England were praying for anybody except themselves, and God and his saints, for the time being, slept.